RETRIBUTION

RETRIBUTION

Porn Star Brothers Book 4

L.J. DIVA

★ Royal Star Publishing ★

Chances is an imprint of Royal Star Publishing
www.royalstarpublishing.com.au

This Collector's Edition paperback published in 2018
All Rights Reserved, Copyright ©L.J. Diva 2018

Trade Paperback ISBN: 978-1-925683-49-3
Case Laminate Hardcover ISBN: 978-1-922307-30-9
E-Book ISBN: 978-1-925683-48-6
A catalogue record for this book is available from the National
Library of Australia.

Cover design: Royal Star Publishing and Odyssey Books
Cover photos: CURAphotography/Shutterstock.com
Typesetting in Minion Pro by Royal Star Publishing

 Dedications

In 2014 a vague idea to write a book about a porn star came to me. In 2015 the idea brewed and grew and when my idol, Jackie Collins, passed away, the idea flourished with a vengeance. Jackie Collins is the only inspiration in my life when it comes to writing. She had the passion, the brains, the ballsy rollicking attitude, and the kind of life that made me want to *be* her. Without her, these books would not exist, for I would not have had the inspiration to follow in the same 'write whatever you want' league. Without her, I will continue trying to write the kind of books she wrote. Real, ballsy, and bonkbustingly good.

Jackie, the Porn Star Brothers book series is dedicated to you as so many of my other books are. I thank you for the inspiration you have given me and hope you continue giving me, to go on and write more. I hope that you are well and having a good laugh wherever you are. I miss you and will continue doing so. Sometimes I think I feel you egging me on with my writing. Maybe that's true, and maybe it's just my rampant imagination; the same imagination that has given me the books I have written so far in my life. And sometimes, I really wished I could be you. You will forever be my idol and inspiration and I thank you. RIP, Miss Jackie C.

And to the three Stefanovic brothers, Carlos, Pedro, and Tomas, without whom I would not have had names for my porn stars.

RETRIBUTION

October 1977

"Pedro, Tomas." Carlos knew his brothers in an instant and ran for them as they did for him. They met in a big group hug. "Oh, my God!" he cried. "You're here, you're here. Are you okay?" He grabbed Pedro's face. "Are you okay? What are you doing here?" He grasped Tomas's shoulder. "What are you doing in America? Oh, my God, how are you?" He engulfed them again.

"What are *we* doing?" Pedro laughed. "What about you?" He hugged his older brothers fiercely, not wanting to let go.

"Oh, God, I've missed the two of you," Tomas mumbled into Carlos's shoulder as he dug his fingers in, not wanting the moment to end. "You've been gone too long, and I missed you both so much."

"Ah, my little brothers," Carlos murmured, longing for their carefree days back on Mykonos. "Where have *I* been? Where have *you* been? Why are you here? *How* are you here?"

"Friends of yours?" Star repeated from behind them.

The boys parted reluctantly. "My brothers," Carlos told Star before noticing the group now standing around them. "And something's clearly going on."

"Detective Gardo, NYPD." The trench-coated six foot Mack Truck sized detective flashed his badge. "We were tracking a man heading for that plane."

"So were we," another trench-coated average height man said. He flashed his badge. "Detective Barden, Miami PD."

"Star, LAPD." He nodded at Drew. "My partner. We were tracking that man." He pointed to the dead body on the tarmac. "Guess he was heading for that plane too."

"Then I guess we have something in common," Gardo said.

"Yeah, like being soaked to the skin," Barden said. "How about we go find somewhere warm and dry to chat, shall we."

With Carlos hanging onto his brothers, and Tony, Aneeka and Mark behind them, they were all shunted into the airport where they were met by security. But all the detectives and officers had to do was flash their badges, of which there were many, and the security guards had no control over the situation. The guards called the manager and showed everyone to a large boardroom where they were given towels and coffee by the girls that arrived along with the manager.

Everyone started talking at once.

"Now, where the hell have you two been?" Carlos demanded, keeping a hand on each of his brothers' shoulders.

"New York."

"Miami."

"Wait a minute." Pedro stopped him. "You don't get away with it that easily. What about you, Mr Hollywood Porn Star with the new hairdo?" His eyes went to his brother's hair. "Why didn't you let us know you were leaving or what you were doing? You just up and left after that shooting."

"You can't talk, little brother," Tomas reminded, eyeing him off and sliding an arm around his own waist as his stomach twinged. "You took off and became a porn star of your own. I saw the pictures."

Carlos watched the two of them. His younger brothers. God, it was so good to see them again. He frowned and looked at Tomas. "Wait. What did you say?" His head turned toward Pedro. "You're in…"

Pedro blushed. "Yeah, yeah. Not that I can talk. It seems I'm following in my big brother's footsteps. I've followed you into the big bad world of pornos."

"Pedro." Carlos's frown was still in place as he took Pedro's face in his hand. "Why?"

Pedro shrugged. "Well, when I saw you doing it, I thought, why not."

"But you're still young. You're only twenty, you have your whole life ahead of you, and that's not you anyway." Carlos's hand slid back to Pedro's shoulder.

Pedro gave a shake of his head. "It's not so bad. My movies are classier, more tasteful, and have better producers." He raised his brows in amusement. "And then I had my own troubles, so back to Carlos since it all started with you. Why did you just up and leave and not let anyone know where you were, or what you were doing?"

Carlos took a deep breath. "I had to. I had to get out of there. I have no idea what the hell that was about."

"What *was* it about?" Tomas asked. "You were called a rapist and murderer. Mama and Papa were sickened by it." He shook his head. "What did *you do,* Carlos?"

"Nothing." Carlos vehemently shook his head. "*I did nothing.* I did *not* rape anyone, and I certainly didn't shoot anyone."

"Then why didn't you stay?" Pedro asked. "Why didn't you stay and fight it?"

"Because I think the gunman was aiming for me and got the woman by mistake. Connie heard the shots, got me inside her room, and told me to meet her by the dock. I raced home and got my stuff and left the letter. Did Mama get the letter? The cops didn't get it did they?"

Two heads shook no.

"Mama got it," Pedro said.

Carlos sighed. "Good," pause, "Connie and Vivian got me out on the ferry to Athens and then on a private jet to L.A. Harry, uh, my new boss, sorted everything out." He turned to Tony who was hovering nearby. "It was all sorted out, wasn't it? Uh, this is Tony, he works for Harry and has been my bodyguard for a few weeks," he told his brothers.

Tony stepped closer. "There was nothing to sort out because it sorted itself out."

Carlos frowned. "What do you mean nothing to sort out?"

"The cops were all over the house," Tomas added.

Tony shrugged. "By the time Harry got me on the case it had been sorted. The cops said it was a case of mistaken identity and a lovers' tiff that had gone awry. You were just in the wrong place at the wrong time."

"If that's the case then, why did all of this happen?" Carlos asked him.

Another shrug. "Dunno," Tony said. "We thought it was a bit strange."

Tomas thought about it. "That's kinda what happened with me. Stuff started in Miami, but all of a sudden it changed gears. I'm brought here, and now this."

Pedro nodded. "Same with me. Now, I'm here." He motioned to Mark. "My bodyguard, Mark Monroe."

Carlos nodded at him and looked around. "Well, there's a hell of a lot of cops for whatever *is* going on, and it all has to do with that plane and who was on it."

"So," Star started as the detectives gathered round. "What have *you* boys been up to and what are your parts in all of this?"

"Searching for a kidnapper," Gardo replied, shrugging off his trench coat and laying it over the closest chair. "Turns out, my kidnapper not only worked for Andros Poulos, the man who was after *my* Stephanopoulos, but someone up the food chain." He downed the remains of his first coffee and picked up another from the tray on the table. "Looks like we got a big fish to fry here somewhere." He looked at Star,

Drew and Barden. "Any ideas?"

Barden shook his head and wrapped his thick cold fingers around his coffee cup for warmth. "I have four dead drug-riddled gay porn stars, a spurned ex-lover, and a flat out raving necrophiliac to deal with, so whoever the guy was that took *my* Stephanopoulos, we found him and ended up shooting him before getting any information." He sipped the hot brew in his cup and let the molten liquid slide down his cold, sore throat.

Gardo raised his brows and grinned. "Is that all you had?" he asked, and Barden wearily grinned back.

Drew sighed, crossed his arms, and half sat beside Barden on the table in the middle of the room. With a glance over his shoulder at the three brothers, he said, "Our Stephanopoulos seems to have caused a hell of a headache. A dead ex-girlfriend, a kidnapped photographer, and two dead henchmen. Ours caused trouble for weeks."

Star snorted. "Is that what you call it?" He called his partner out. "That little cock sucker has been the bane of my existence for weeks, and that's more than *mere trouble.*" He shifted position and snarled across the room at the brothers, slamming his hands onto his hips as the rest of the cops and Feds hovered around the table, chatting and warming themselves with coffee and blankets. "He's a little cock sucker that needs to be taught a lesson."

Drew warily eyed his partner. He'd never seen him so angry over anyone, but the last few weeks had turned Star into some sort of raving maniac out for revenge on everybody.

Gardo's eyes narrowed. He knew types like Star. Hot-headed like himself, but also angry and full of resentment at his lot in life and the fact minorities and people who didn't seem to work hard for anything always got more than him. Arrogance, narcissism, and self-loathing all rolled into one. Cops like Star thought the world owed them and got pissed off when it didn't deliver.

Barden stayed quiet. He was a people watcher from way back, and after flying around in the freezing fall winds and rain during the investigation, he was running low on energy. And Star was not someone he wanted to get into a row with when he was not running at his peak. He knew better than to confront men like Star, knew to stay out of their way and let them self-destruct all in their own time.

Just down the side of the room from his seat at the table, a black-suited Fed eyed everyone. He was a trained profiler, and knew exactly what everyone in that room was just by reading their body language, and hearing the words out of their mouths.

Well, now, let me see, he thought. *The three brothers have no idea what's going on as their actions and speech portray. They're hugging and holding and speaking and acting like they haven't seen each other in the months they've been apart. Their body language speaks of nothing else but truth, some fear, and an utter lack of information.*

The two men standing behind them are stoic, hard-backed, like they have a rod up their ass, military trained maybe. Trained in more than that, martial arts, know how to handle guns and deal with crazed people. But how did two kidnappers get past them? His eyes travelled up and down Tony and Mark who caught him out when they stared back. He smiled slightly, knowing full well they knew what he was and did. So they hardened even more against his eyeball invasion. *They're good,* he thought. *They would probably hold up well against torture techniques.*

His gaze roamed around the room to the many cops there as part of their job, having tagged along in the three car chases for the kidnappers. They had hung around to see those cases out until the end. *And that's all they're doing,* he surmised, watching two officers called Burns and Devron in particular. *But they're making mental notes. Look at the way their eyes are taking everything in. They're watching everyone closely, studying body language and listening to words being said. Yes,* he thought, *those two want to go somewhere and be something, and they're on the lookout for it.* He eyed Devron's six feet of hard-muscled blackness. *Not sure he'll get far being gay, though, closeted or not. But I think he'll give it a damn good go.*

And then there were the detectives. They were only there to claim a win. With one in particular, Star, there for the glory only. He knew men like Star, and he needed to be told by a higher authority, not that that always stopped him. *Like now,* he thought. *He's been threatened with suspension over this case and yet has doggedly gone after the criminal with every ounce of anger he has.*

The suit eyed Star up and down. *He may be good at what he does, but he can be a son of a bitch doing it. And his poor partner Drew. A weak man, or maybe polite and well-mannered are the words for him. Rarely let's his temper flare and is always stopping Star from making a mistake. Sadly for you, though,* the suit scratched his chin, *it could be the downfall of your career unless you stop partnering him.*

Then there was Gardo, who knew his position in life and had worked damn hard for it. His size and bulk held him in good stead and helped make him what he was. A formidable opponent when it came to crime. He knew all about Gardo's track record. And a damn good one it was. Nine out of ten crims caught and the only real one not yet captured was Nedro Scarvo. The suit took a sip of coffee. *The one criminal so many cops wanted, and Gardo was yet to catch. I doubt he's going to let retirement stop him from trying.*

And Jeremiah Barden is a slow burner. He spent his years working his way up dealing with Miami crime, and now the gay scene that's currently thriving. Four dead porn stars and a necrophiliac! How I'd love to help him with that one.

His attention turned to the stunning African American woman walking into the room. *Now,* he thought, *how does she figure into things?* He liked women of style and class, and this one had it, even if she was a Negro. It didn't matter to him. While he'd never been with a black woman before, he had no qualms in admiring the beauty of them. And this one was definitely a beauty. Regal, tall, slim, and in control of every man around her.

His head swung back at the mutterings down the table and saw the black fury sweep over Star's face as he stared at the woman across the room, hands on hips, brows so far down they were joined between his eyes. *Ah, look at that. The anger, hatred, and resentment are so evident, and then there are all those other things I'd like to get into,* he thought. His eyes swung from Star's facial expression to watch the woman approach the brothers.

"Carlos, I've just called Harry to let him know we are safe. Vivian was there as well." Aneeka came up behind the three brothers.

Carlos turned to her. "Thanks for that. I can't wait to see Viv again."

"I'm sure she feels the same way," Aneeka replied warmly, looking the boys up and down.

"Boys, this is—"

"Aneeka Ne Masta, one of the best photographers in the world." Pedro reached out to shake her hand. "Pleasure."

"And it is a pleasure to see such good genetics run in the family." She shook hands with both brothers. "No wonder you're all famous."

"All?" Carlos asked. "Who?" He turned to Tomas with a crestfallen expression. *"Not you, too?"*

Tomas blushed softly, a small smile coming to his lips. "I found my way into it through someone I met."

"Ah, Jesus, Tomas!" Carlos managed before being interrupted.

"All right, all right, listen up porn brothers," Star yelled over the commotion, thinking he could *and would* take control of the whole situation. For that was what Star's personality was all about. Being in control. And when he wasn't…look out. Carlos frowned at the phrasing as Star continued. "We've all had a little chat, now we wanna hear from you three. From the beginning, shall we." He downed his coffee and slammed the cup onto the table.

Carlos sighed and looked around the room. There were cops, Feds and detectives. He leant against the edge of the cupboard behind him with Pedro and Tomas to his right, all three of them standing with their arms crossed.

Aneeka, Tony and Mark stood to his left.

"I have no idea how this started except that someone wanted to frame me for the murder of a friend," Carlos started.

"I meant," Star interrupted with an impatient wave of his hand. "*The beginning.* As in, that little rape and murder crime you were wanted for, but somehow, *someway,* the case suddenly disappeared, and it's all a case of mistaken identity. Start from Mykonos and go from there."

Carlos's frown deepened. *Where the hell is this going, and what does it have to do with what's happening now?*

"Same goes for you two." Star pointed to Pedro and Tomas. "One at a time."

The brothers exchanged looks.

With another sigh, Carlos started again. "I was a

masseur by night and was on to my second customer when the previous customer suddenly popped up and called my current customer a whore and asked *how could she?* I turned and saw a man with a gun with the woman, and took off running when the gun went off."

"Masseur, huh?" Star harrumphed almost triumphantly, so ready to burn the porn star to the ground with his attitude. "You were *more* than a masseur. You were a cock for sale. You fucked the women for money." His contempt was evident, and so was his 'I've got him now' grin. His eyes quickly went around the room to see that his fellow officers were watching the porn star with interest. *Oh, I've so got him,* he thought.

Carlos burned with fury inside. "So what if I did?" he snapped. "Are you *jealous* of my ten inch cock and the amount of women it's had, detective? Or the fact I get paid thousands to fuck hundreds of women you can only *dream* of fucking yourself?"

Snickers went through the room, and Star reddened like a sun-drenched tomato, growing redder still when his fellow detectives joined in the laughter with sidelong glances and sniggers.

"Either way," Carlos continued, seeing his discomfort. "There *was* no rape, and I *didn't shoot anyone.*"

"How did you get off Mykonos?" Barden asked from his spot on the table where he sat sideways so he could see all three brothers. He marvelled how a half Greek could not look Greek. Unlike his brothers, Carlos had no visible Greek in him whatsoever.

"I had help from friends," Carlos told him. "They got me on the ferry, then on a plane to Hollywood, and I stayed with one of them for a while."

"What happened then?" Gardo straightened his blazer and shifted closer to Barden. He wanted his own clear view of the brothers so he could try and figure out how one little boy called Pedro could get himself into so much trouble. And now he was finding out it had to do with his two older brothers. *Ah,* Gardo thought. *That's brotherly love for ya. The family that plays together, and gets involved with crime together, stays together.*

"Everything was supposedly taken care of by my new boss, and things were fine until the day I went into Rosalee's house. I had called her about having lunch, and she said she wanted me to come over. I did and found her naked. We had sex, and I got hit over the head with something. When I came to I was tied to a chair, and there was a man having sex with her, another was standing to my right, watching. They made me watch her being raped then they injected her and hit me over the head again. I blacked out and came to when the sirens were coming, and I stumbled out the back door and over to Aneeka's."

"I knew that fence wasn't a gardening accident," Star yelled across the room, surprising everyone as he pointed his thick, calloused accusatory forefinger at her.

Aneeka didn't move except for one brow that arched itself into position. "Very astute of you, *detective.*"

His eyes narrowed at the insult, and his hands

moved for his hips. He knew from psychology training that to make yourself look bigger and more threatening you put your hands on your hips and puff your chest out. Clearly, that didn't work on this woman. And he hated it.

"I slept most of the day and came up with a story to tell you," Carlos went on, ignoring Star and his childish tantrums. "After that, Aneeka was broken into, *I* was broken into, then Aneeka was kidnapped and so was I. And now we're here." Carlos spread his hands. "With thirty or so cops and Feds and my brothers involved."

"Okay, that's your story. Pedro, tell everyone yours," Gardo said and grabbed another coffee and a sandwich.

Pedro glanced at his brothers before starting. "I didn't think too much *was* happening. I worked in a club on Santorini for Andros Poulos. He owned it. All I was doing was minding my own business, and then I found out I was being drugged. He had his assistant put it into my drinks when I was working."

"Pedro," Carlos said. "Are you all right? You didn't keep taking them, did you? Mama and Papa didn't raise us to do drugs."

"I know, I know," Pedro replied with a small wave of his hand, blushing and hating being chastised by his older brother in front of so many cops. "I didn't know he was doing it, but when I found out, I stopped drinking anything they brought me." He shook his head. "I ended up sleeping with his daughter, and he found out. He threatened to kill me, but Angelina hit him over the head, and we took off for Athens and went on to New York where she was going to be attending Juilliard. Everything was okay until he attacked Angie. She took a restraining order out on him and he was arrested and charged. I crashed my car and ended up in the hospital with cops telling me they had found drugs in my car."

He glanced around the room as Carlos stood a little straighter and turned towards him. "Turns out Andros had set me up, stashing the drugs and cutting my brakes so I'd have the accident. After that, we found out I had a stalker, she jumped in my new car and drove it into Andros Poulos and killed him. That's the last thing I saw before being shoved into the trunk of a car by a guy with a gun. I managed to escape and was picked up by you and Mark." He motioned to Gardo and his bodyguard. "We made our way here, and now here we are with my brothers, finding out all about what actually happened."

"It seemed Andros Poulos was in cahoots with Nedro Scarvo, Long Island's resident drug kingpin. One of his cohorts was the one who stashed the drugs," Gardo said. "And then there was the guy who worked for Andros Poulos. He grabbed the kid, and we followed him here to Chicago, not knowing where he was going or what he was doing. He didn't make it to the plane. He was killed when they found the kid had escaped."

"Yeah, well," Star muttered, leaning on the back of a chair and crossing his legs as he stood beside his peers. "So was ours, join the club. Next."

Everyone stared at Tomas who glanced around at

all of the eyes staring at him.

"That's you, lover boy," Star added.

Tomas blushed and cleared his throat. "I was a personal trainer at the same resort Carlos worked at. After both he and Pedro had left, I decided to pack my bags and leave as well. Some of the guests I trained lived in Miami and they offered me a place to stay and help to get my career off the ground. So after getting involved with someone I shouldn't have, I moved there and was immediately welcomed with open arms. After a few weeks, I met Roger who…" He briefly glanced at his brothers with a slight movement of his head. "Introduced me to the world of porn."

Carlos groaned. "Oh, God, I really can't believe you too."

Tomas kept going, but he was rapidly declining in every way, shape and form, especially his breathing and strength. "Everything was going well. We moved in together and were making movies, but things were happening. Roger's car was damaged by some vandal, things were stolen from the studio, and then other actors were being killed off. Roger was fingered—"

"I'm sure he was," Star muttered.

Tomas reddened and shifted uncomfortably. "And he was arrested. I'd been feeling unwell for a few days and collapsed. I ended up in the hospital, and that's when I was kidnapped and taken away. The rest is hazy because I was so sick, but I ended up here at the airport with Barden pulling me out of a car and telling me what had happened. Turns out, a guy I met on Mykonos decided to kill off anyone I worked with or got involved with. As for the other guy, I have no idea who he was or what he wanted." He noticed Pedro looking at him strangely and frowned, feeling his stomach lurch.

"Tomas, are you okay now? You don't look so good." Carlos leant past Pedro, to intently examine his brother's face.

Tomas swallowed and blinked slowly. "I'm weak, but okay. I think. Apparently, my milk was poisoned, and I was slowly ingesting it day by day. I got the cure in the hospital. I'll be okay…I hope…" His strength slipped further, and his breathing laboured.

"We need to get you checked out again after the ordeal you went through," Carlos said, reaching out to him. He turned to the cops. "Can we get a doctor to check him over?"

Barden nodded. "I'll get the airport doctor in."

Carlos thought about it. "All three of us have been set up for, or affected by, crimes we didn't commit. What the hell is going on? Because clearly, *something is* going on?"

The black-suited man finally stood. "My name is Special Agent Payday from the FBI." He flashed his badge around. "I suggest you gentlemen," he told the four detectives, "tell your stories now." He put his badge away and waited.

Star rolled his eyes at the interruption from some FBI bigwig that had nothing to do with it. "I suppose I'll go first. We first caught wind of Carlos Stephanopoulos when we were called to a house. We found the body of Rosalee Brentworth on her bed, naked, injected, surrounded by drugs. Her place was turned over, there was no sign of a break and enter, and the only two things out of place was the broken side fence to Ms Ne Masta's house and the car parked out front. This we found out belonged to Mr Stephanopoulos. Ms Ne Masta gave us a detailed description of the two men she had seen in Ms Brentworth's backyard, and we found Mr Stephanopoulos at her house the next day. We kept a tail on him, as well as the two men."

He shifted position to make himself look like the most important man in the room. "But we found these men to be using aliases to hire cars, motel rooms, etc. We wanted to link one of them to several assaults that happened, but had no hard evidence. We did get one of their prints and photo, plus a passport and ID when he was arrested for indecent exposure just down the road from Mr Stephanopoulos's. His name was Dimitri Yustoff. We kept an even closer eye on them then. Not long after, we followed the men to the Venice Beach Pier where we arrested Mr Vega for interfering in a sting operation."

Tony mumbled under his breath. He moved and sneered at Star, flexing the biceps of his tightly crossed arms.

Star snidely glanced at Tony. "*He* informed us that Ms Ne Masta and Mr Stephanopoulos had been kidnapped. Once we had details and put out an all-points bulletin, an off-duty cop spotted Dimitri Yustoff on the highway to Vegas, and we followed. All the way here to O'Hare. Clearly, he was catching a flight. Clearly, they didn't want to wait for him. And now here we are." He spread his hands. "Wasting our time sharing when we could be catching them at the other end."

"Do you know which company that plane was registered to, or who *owns* the company?" Payday asked, knowing what the answer would be.

Star's face reddened. "No, not yet."

"Well, *we do,* so wait your turn," Payday said, sliding his hands into his pockets. "Gardo, you're next."

Gardo put down his coffee cup and stood. He'd been sitting through the boys' explanations and Star's diatribe and now took centre stage. Burns and Devron were behind him, ready to back up the story and add their bit if needed. "Mr Stephanopoulos first came to our attention after the assault on Angelina Poulos. Her father had done the deed, but blamed the kid, clearly wanting him to go to jail so he was free and clear. But Angelina filed charges and Poulos was arrested. After that, we had the drugs and cut brakes, plus the shooting outside of *Studio 69,* New York's hottest nightclub where Mr Stephanopoulos works as the resident DJ. He was standing with Angelina and another woman when a car drove by and a shot was fired. Both women were injured, but survived. Mr Stephanopoulos got away scratch free."

Carlos looked sharply at his brother. "You forgot to mention that!"

Pedro had the decency to look sheepish. "Did I?" He nonchalantly shrugged a shoulder at his scowling brother.

"We kept an eye on Mr Stephanopoulos and found out he had a stalker who then proceeded to kill Poulos the other night outside of 69. He was kidnapped by our small time crook in those few moments, and we followed them here to Chicago, but we couldn't track down his name, although, I guess we will now. A very tangled web it all was, and I'm sure, *still* is." He grabbed another coffee from the fresh tray of drinks the airport staff brought around. "Someone is definitely out to get you boys."

Payday spoke up. "Barden, your turn."

Jeremiah Barden straightened from his spot on the table and slowly glanced at every face of every person in the room as he spoke. "Tomas Stephanopoulos first came to our attention when we were called to Marcus Seralift's home for a dead body. A porn star, dead of a suspected overdose, which was nothing unusual. What *was* unusual is that it was the first of many. Three more actors from *Seralift Productions* all died in the same way, and *all* had their fingers pointed at Mr Roger Dencott, Mr Stephanopoulos' partner *on* screen and in real life."

Devron's interest perked up at that tidbit of information, and he eyed Tomas with renewed interest. A *gay* Greek God. *Mmm, the Greeks are definitely tasty looking indeed,* he thought as his lips laid themselves on a fresh cup of coffee he imagined was hot hard Greek cock. *Pedro's tall and white and gorgeous, but Tomas is dark and brooding and gay. Just the way I like them.*

Pedro and Carlos turned their heads to look at Tomas who reddened. He clenched his jaw, and his eyes swept the floor. His sexuality had never been discussed with his family, and it was embarrassing for them to find out this way. Not to mention all the cops who were staring. His jaw clenched harder, and he hugged himself tighter.

"It came to the chase when the fourth body was left in the underground car park to their apartment. I arrested Dencott for it, and Stephanopoulos collapsed in my station. He was rushed to the hospital and we found he had been poisoned. I managed to put two and two together and realised his milk was what had been tampered with. We rushed it to the hospital for analysis, and he was given the drug to counteract it. That's when Luiz Manning took him from the hospital and absconded with him. We found Manning's body in a seedy hotel room with a bullet through the forehead. Stephanopoulos was gone, but after a report from a guy at a gas station hearing someone in a trunk yelling for help, *and* seeing the driver flash his gun, I knew it was them and followed them here to Chicago. I kept track on the radio and heard about the other boys and what was going on. We found Tomas not long before the rest of you got here. We had to shoot our guy dead as he tried to make his getaway." He glanced at the other detectives with a cocked brow. "All three brothers kidnapped and brought here to Chicago. Coincidence times three?"

"Tomas," Carlos said quietly. "Are you all right now?" He reached across Pedro to squeeze his brother's arm, but Tomas swiftly moved past him and walked out the door.

"Tomas?" Carlos said in surprise, standing. Glancing back at everyone he said, "Let's take a break, he's clearly still not well." He followed him out the door with Pedro hot on his heels. They found Tomas halfway down the hallway leaning against the wall, breathing heavily and looking quite sick.

"Tomas," Carlos called. "Are you still feeling sick? You need to see a doctor. What about having some food and drink? That might make you feel better." But one look at his brother's shame-filled burning face and he knew exactly what it was about. He softened and held Tomas's face in his hands. "Oh…Tomas. Are you okay? Because *it's* okay." Shaking his head, he added, "I always wondered. You weren't into girls, but I was never sure if you were into boys either."

Tomas's face crumpled into tears and he slid down the wall until he was crouching. Wrapping his arms around his head, he sobbed.

"Tomas." Carlos went down to the floor and held his brother tight with Pedro right there beside him.

"It's all been a lot for you, being poisoned and all. You must still be so weak and sick. Maybe you need to go back to the hospital to make sure you're okay." He rubbed his brother's back. "As for being gay, that's okay. We don't hate you, we don't anything. You're our brother, we love you." He kissed his head and pulled back.

Tomas rubbed his hands over his face and through his hair. "I've never mentioned anything, never said, never thought, but Mama…"

"*She* knows?" Pedro asked, sliding his arm around Tomas's shoulder.

"I told her," Tomas said, finally looking up. "She…

She was okay with it after a few moments, but Papa…"

"Does *he* know?" Carlos asked.

Tomas shook his head. "I didn't tell him, and I doubt Mama has but…oh, God, if he finds out… What will he do? We're Greek. Greek men aren't gay, they're manly and masculine and straight." He replicated their father's words. "How many times have we heard stuff like that over the last few years?"

"I'm sure Mama will bring Papa round," Carlos said. "Once they find out we're all alive and healthy it will be okay." His smile was lopsided. "This Roger guy, does he make you happy?"

A bright smile slowly lit up Tomas's face. "Yes."

Carlos smiled and nodded. "Good, *but*…what about the person you were involved with but shouldn't have been? And this Luiz Manning? Are they the same…? What…?" He swallowed. "What was going on there?"

The smile disappeared from Tomas's face and he closed his eyes. "Yes, they're the same person. Luiz was…my first…I didn't know who he was, just that I was intensely attracted to him." His head bowed, ashamed of the whole thing. "I only found out after it happened…that he was engaged to one of my clients, and I vowed to end it…but he followed me out to one of the islands and we…" He shuddered. "We spent the weekend together. I didn't want it to end, but I knew what I was doing was wrong, and so I confessed the whole thing to Bertha St John who told me she knew all about his bisexuality and that we should both dump him."

Ragged laughter tore from his throat. "I saw him

once in Miami before I met Roger, then once more when we had a coffee at a café. Then all of the murders, and Roger getting arrested, and me getting sick…I never for the life of me thought it was *him* doing it." He glanced up under hooded eyes. "I never thought anything like that would ever happen."

Carlos kissed the top of his head. "Well, it's over now. He's dead, and you're with a man you love. Does he treat you well?"

Tomas lifted his head, a silly smile on his face. "Yeah. Yeah, he does. I love him so much." His emotions flowed over his face like a waterfall, and he heaved a breath.

Carlos saw those emotions and nodded. "Good. I can't wait to meet him."

Tomas suddenly frowned. "Oh, my God, I should call him. I wonder if Barden has had him released yet."

"I have." Barden walked up to them, and the boys helped a weary Tomas stand. "Just now during the break. I told them to hold him there because I'd let you know and you might want to call. But right now, you're needed back inside."

They walked back into the room, supporting Tomas as they went, and stood where they had before.

"So…" Payday stood when he saw them enter and walked over to a whiteboard on the end wall where he picked up a black marker to start laying out the issues. "What we have here is a case of connect the dots."

He drew three circles down the left side of the board. "We have three brothers. All accused of crimes or connected to them. All attacked by thugs." He drew three smaller circles to represent the thugs to the right of the first three and drew connecting lines.

"What we know is, someone pulled off all three crimes against the boys, but we don't know who." He drew a big circle on the right side of the board.

"We know that all of the thugs involved were coming here to Chicago to catch a plane." He drew a plane and connected lines to the thugs. "Do they work for someone? Do they work for the same company? Did they know each other? Did they all complete their missions? No. What we *do* know is that plane is registered to Brickam West Imports here in Chicago."

He drew a circle to the right of the plane and wrote the initials BWI in it then added a connecting line. "What we know is that company is owned by Freeman Imports, a global company that operates around the world." He drew another circle to the right with the initials FI and another line. "What we know is Freeman Imports is owned by Papadopoulos Exports in Athens, Greece, and that is owned by Stefano Papadopoulos who lives in Athens." He finished connecting the dots and added the initials SP to the large circle on the far right of the board.

Carlos frowned. Where had he heard that name before?

"And who's Stefano Papadopoulos?" Star asked, his arms going from his hips to being crossed in front of him. He hated being out of the loop and his arrogance over the matter had gotten the best of him.

"A very wealthy businessman with many pies containing many fingers," Payday said, putting the marker down and brushing off his hands. "We've been looking into him for some time."

"What for?" Gardo asked. "Does he run mobs? Drugs?"

"All of the above and then some." Payday walked back to his seat at the table and grasped the back of his chair. "We have managed to track down every limb of the tree, the *family* tree, from Papadopoulos." He stared at Pedro. "To Andros Poulos, who, at one stage, was his stepson."

Pedro glared back in surprise. "What?"

"Yes." Payday returned the look. "I couldn't believe it either, especially when I just put it all together during the break."

"What together?" Star asked, now downing his fifth coffee. He needed another toilet break and was getting pissed off that he wasn't up to speed because some FBI twat wasn't telling him anything except when making a grand declaration to the whole room.

Payday tried to hide his amusement. *Ah, men like Star. Arrogant assholes who think they know it all.* "That Papadopoulos is also connected to the murder of Luiz Manning in Miami. You know why?" He watched Tomas. "Because Luiz was Andros's illegitimate son that he never claimed."

That surprised Tomas, and he stood a little straighter.

"And finally…" He turned to Carlos. "Papadopoulos is behind getting the charges against *you* dropped. Apparently, the shooter was taken care of. Not to mention the kidnapping."

"But why would he do that?" Carlos asked. "We

don't know anyone by the name of Papadopoulos. Why would he get us out of our legal troubles?"

"Are *you sure* you don't know him?" Payday asked, searching his face intently. "There must be *some* connection somewhere?"

"If there is I don't know it," Carlos snapped and rubbed his head. "The name is vaguely familiar, like I've heard it somewhere, but can't place it."

"Think, damn it!" Star thumped his large fist on the table. "If you're caught up in this—"

"Enough!" Payday yelled, and Star stopped and stared. "*You're not in charge* Detective Star. *None* of you are. Whereas *I am.*"

"But I—" Star started.

"Are just a cop, and *I'm* an FBI agent," Payday said. "*I* have jurisdiction."

The pain was banging around in Carlos's head like a hammer. "Ugh, I can't think."

"You have to," Payday went on as he turned back to him. "Whatever you know, or have heard, *we need* to know it too."

Everyone in the room was staring at him, muttering, focussing their attention. Star was giving him the evil eye. Gardo and Barden were watching. Payday was staring intensely. It was all too much. "No, I can't, not here, not now. My head is killing me." He dropped the towel from around his shoulders and stormed out of the room.

Tony moved after him, but Aneeka stopped him. "Let me," she told the room. "He needs a few minutes of peace and quiet." Tony nodded, and she followed

Carlos down the hall to the floor-to-ceiling window. "It was too much for you to handle in that room." Her voice was low and soothing.

Carlos sighed. The pounding had subsided with the quiet. "Yes, too much."

She massaged his neck and the back of his head. "Just relax," she soothed. "Let it all go. Let the stress leave your body. The tiredness, the fear, the problems. Let it all go. Let it all wash away on a wave of warm salty ocean. Warm and soft and enveloping you as you float along."

Carlos breathed deeply and let everything go.

"Remember back," Aneeka went on. "Remember the voice, the person, whoever it was. Wherever it was that you heard the name, Papadopoulos. Just listen to the name being said and let your mind remember everything else around it."

Carlos's mind drifted back.

"Papadopoulos you have no right to be here. I owe you nothing. Get out of my shop and don't come back."

"You don't get to tell me what to do Stephanopoulos. You're just a lowlife little scum at the bottom of the pool. I have more, I own more, I am more than you'll ever be."

"And I don't care."

"No, you wouldn't. You have your foreign wife and your half-breed sons—"

"Don't you ever call my children that!"

"Or what? You'll kill me?"

"I won't need to."

Silence.

"What does that mean?"

"It means that I won't be the one to deal with you… He never liked you, in fact, he hated you."

"Are you threatening me…with him?"

"Do I need to?"

The meat store formed in Carlos's mind. He'd been seventeen, working one afternoon when his father had a visitor at the back door. He'd never seen who it was, but definitely heard the voice.

"He won't do anything to help you and your half-breed—"

Thwack!

The thud was heard through the store making Carlos jump. He knew his father had just slammed his meat cleaver into one of the wood boards on the table out back.

"I told you not to call my sons that."

Silence.

"Mmm…well don't get on the wrong side of me, Stephanopoulos. You won't win."

"Neither will you."

Carlos's eyes flew open, and there was a sharp intake of breath. Turning on his heel, he sped down the hallway to his brothers who were standing there waiting, huddled together for warmth and comfort and support.

"What's going on?" they asked together.

"We're leaving," Carlos replied.

"Where are we going?" Their expressions showed their surprise and curiosity.

"Home!"

"And where would home be these days?" Payday asked as the detectives gathered in the doorway.

"Mykonos," Carlos said. "We're going home tonight. But we need a private plane, no names, and we can't land in Athens."

"Why not?" Payday asked, intrigued by the sudden change in plans and Carlos's behaviour. Clearly, something was going on.

Carlos stared at him. "Because *he* can't know we're home…and we also don't have our passports."

"All right, what's going on?" Star demanded. "Who do you think you are, giving the orders?" He slammed his hands onto his hips as was his habit.

"*He's* not," Payday told the hostile Star. "*I* am." He now turned to his men. "Get a private plane ready. We'll fly into Mykonos. Tell no one. No names, no credentials. Nothing."

"Who do you think—" Star started with a waving finger.

"The FBI," Payday told him before encompassing the rest of the group. "The rest of you are dismissed. You can all head back to your hometowns. The FBI has official control of this case. We'll keep your captains informed of what's happening so you can close your cases." After a moment of confused, but relieved expressions, he turned back to Carlos. "Tell me why Mykonos? Why home? You remember something; you remember where you heard the name."

Carlos glanced at the others then beckoned Payday down the hallway out of earshot. "Seven years ago I was working in my father's meat shop when someone turned up at the back door. My father said his name, Papadopoulos, and then he threatened my father. But they also mentioned a *he*. No name, just *he*." Carlos shrugged. "I think we should go home on the sly and find out from my father, then go and see Papadopoulos to find out what's going on."

Payday nodded thoughtfully. "One step at a time. We'll get to Mykonos then Athens. But first…" He looked down at Carlos. "We need to make sure you blend in with us." They walked back to the others where Star, Drew, Gardo, Barden and Payday's men were waiting. "Take these boys to the menswear store and get them suits, they need to look like us, and I'll call the doctor in to check on this one." He pointed to Tomas, and his men nodded and led them away.

Aneeka stepped up to Payday and spoke with the natural allure she always used to get what she wanted from men. "We will be going too, Agent Payday, but we also don't have our passports, money, clothes or bags. Will the FBI be gracious enough to pay for the things *we* need?"

Payday generously eyed her up and down then gave Mark and Tony a cold once over as they were of no real interest to him. "Go and get some things from the pharmacy and a change of clothes. We'll foot the bill."

She smiled graciously, gave a nod of her head, and held his hand between both of hers as thanks. "Thank you, Special Agent Payday. Thank you very much." Turning on her heel, she took off for the pharmacy.

Tony and Mark stayed. Turns out, they knew

something of each other, and while they had never met, had heard many stories of past battles.

"Do you know who Carlos works for?" Tony asked Payday.

"And Pedro?" Mark added.

"Harry DeVille and Greta Von Burro along with Marcus Seralift are the porn kings and queen of the business." *Ah yes,* Payday thought. *I know all about them.*

"Harry wants me here all the way, protecting his asset, so I'll be coming," Tony said.

"And Pedro hired me personally, so I'm in," Mark added.

Payday nodded. "I don't like it, but then if they have the two of you to protect them, we won't need to."

Tony and Mark nodded. "That's our job."

*****

After towelling down and being fitted for a suit, Pedro took a few minutes to phone Angelina. "Babe, it's me. I'm in Chicago. I'm okay."

"Oh, my God, Pedro," Angelina cried down the line. "I was so scared. I haven't heard anything. The police haven't called me, and Sara-Michelle hasn't heard from Mark, although, she's on the phone now. I didn't know if you were alive or dead or okay…" she sobbed.

"Angie," he murmured. "I'm okay. But I can't come home to New York yet. We need to go home to Mykonos to sort this shit out. Something big is going on and the cops, and Feds, and FBI are involved. And you'll never guess what. Carlos and Tomas are here as well. Someone wants to cause trouble for all of us, and this needs to be dealt with. The FBI are taking us home to sort it out."

"Oh, God, back home. I want to come. Please don't say no. I love you. I need to come over there."

"Look, I have no idea what's going to happen." Pedro glanced over his shoulder to look around the airport. The phones were about twenty feet from the men's shop, and Mark and Tony had arrived to keep an eye on them. "I know Carlos's friend Aneeka is coming; she's getting a hotel room in Athens, paid for by the FBI no less, and she told me to give the address to you and to wait for her there if you decided to come."

"Oh, that's good." Angelina sighed. "There's so much I have to tell you. To *say* to you. I love you, and I never want to be apart again."

"I never want to be apart from you. I love you, Angie. I'll see you in a day or two in Athens. If you don't hear from me don't worry, we'll be taking care of business. It's the *Elegance Hotel*, and ask for Aneeka Ne Masta. And can you bring my passport, papers and money, and a suitcase with clothes?"

"Okay, I'll bring everything. I love you."

"I love you, too. Bye." He hung up and saw Tomas with his back to him on the other phone. He gave his shoulder a quick squeeze as he walked past.

Tomas acknowledged Pedro's touch and nervously twirled the phone cord around his fingers. "Roger, it's me. Are you okay?"

"Me! What about you? You were in the hospital sick and dying. Are you okay? Have you seen a doctor? How do you feel? Are you hurt? Did that bastard do anything to you I know it was Luiz who killed off our friends and tried to set me up for their murders the lying stinking bastard." He finally took a breath.

"I'm fine," Tomas interrupted, feeling the burn of passion for the man he loved being so worried about him. "A bit weak and woozy, but the doctor's going to check me over in a minute. Look, the reason I'm calling, besides to hear your voice, is that we have to go home to Mykonos. Carlos and Pedro are here with me, you'd never guess what the hell's going on in a million years, but it's very confusing, and there's too much going on to explain it all over the phone."

"Do you want me to fly over?" Roger asked. "I can pack a case for you and bring it with me."

"That would be great, and bring my passport and legal papers. I may need them. A friend of Carlos is getting a hotel room in Athens that you can go to. I don't know how long this will take, or what it's about, or who's involved, so ask for her at the counter."

"Okay, let me just get a pad and pen…okay, give it to me."

"It's the *Elegance Hotel* in Athens under the name Aneeka Ne Masta."

"The famous photographer?"

"Yeah, we'll all meet up there." He glanced up and saw Carlos waving him over. "I gotta go. I love you."

"Love you too."

"Bye." Tomas hung up and went for his fitting.

An hour later, they were boarding a private jet for Mykonos. Aneeka, Tony and Mark took seats across the aisle from the boys who looked remarkably different in suits and ties. Their hair was slicked down, and they had dark glasses to conceal their identities. It was going to be a very long flight, and they had much to catch up on.

"So…" Carlos directed a stare at Pedro. "Angelina?"

A goofy smile spread across Pedro's face. "Yeah."

Carlos laughed. "Are you in lurve?" he teased.

Pedro's smile got bigger. "Yeah."

"Is it serious?" Tomas asked. He'd never seen his brother serious about any girl, and no girl had put a grin like that on his face before. But then he *was* only twenty.

The smile spread from ear to ear. "Yeah…what about you? Is it serious with Roger?"

Tomas frowned slightly then thought about Roger, and the same goofy Stephanopoulos grin spread across his face. "Yeah," he said softly.

Pedro's head moved up and down. "Finally, our brother is happy with someone. It was a long time coming, bro. We didn't think it was *ever* gonna happen. Guess we just needed to let you figure it all out on your own. Especially *who* you were going to be with."

Tomas looked into his brother's eyes. "Yeah, it took a while. But I found him."

"Good," Pedro said then turned to Carlos. "Now, big bro, who the hell is Viv?"

Carlos blushed.

"Ooohhh," Pedro teased. "*Clearly* someone special.

A girlfriend? A lover? A wife?" Carlos looked up sharply, and Pedro leant forward in his seat. "Oh, my God, she's not your wife, is she? Did you get married and not tell Mama and Papa or us?"

Carlos sighed and waved his hand. "No, little brother. I didn't get married...but..." He thought about Viv and felt the heaving of love in his chest. "She is *definitely* someone very special indeed."

"Serious?" Tomas asked from his seat next to him.

"Very," Carlos replied, his gaze drifting out the window.

"Very." Pedro leant back. He was sitting facing them and watched Carlos's face. "It really *is* serious. Just look at the loved-up expression on his face," he told Tomas. "*Very* loved-up indeed."

"Just can it and let's get down to business." Carlos pointed a finger at Pedro. "*Your* story from start to finish and don't leave anything out. I can't wait to hear how *you* got into the porn industry."

Pedro sat back and stuck his feet up on the armrest between his brothers. When they stared disdainfully at his feet, he said, "Hey, it's gonna be a long story."

Half an hour later, Carlos was shaking his head. "Pedro, Pedro, Pedro. You always did get yourself into trouble, and fucking the boss's daughter was what started it all off."

Pedro shrugged. "I couldn't help it. I was high on drugs, and she was offering herself to me...I took her and *kept* on taking her. Besides, she's hot and gorgeous, and I love her."

"Did she encourage you to start in the business, or

are you still using me as an excuse?" Carlos asked.

Pedro shrugged and pulled a face. "If you can do it why can't I? Besides, it pays well, and I get to do what you do, write my scripts and earn more money."

"Is that what you *are* doing, or what you'll *be* doing and *still* using me as an excuse for it?" Carlos joked.

"Who knows?" Pedro grinned. "Maybe *one* day I'll stop using you as an excuse. One day when I'm old and grey and have more money than you. Like I have a bigger cock than you." The expression on his face was cockier than the tone of his voice.

"Ouch," Tomas said with a glance at Carlos. "Burn."

"Yeah, yeah," Carlos grumbled. "Not funny." He changed the direction of the conversation. "I still can't believe Barbara Weston turned her psycho attentions to you. After what she did to me, Papa hit her with a legal letter. But clearly, that didn't stop her."

"Yeah." Pedro moved his head up and down. "That was some pretty weird shit. What she did to me on the beach in Santorini, moving on to Angelina and what she did to her. The gifts she sent were seriously sick. But less about me and more about Tomas." He turned his attention to his brother.

Tomas shook his head. "Uh-uh. Let's hear about Carlos's time in Hollywood." He turned *his* attention to his older brother. "Let's hear how you won the best cock award."

Carlos groaned. "It's all a part of the industry as you boys will soon find out. Has the world seen what you have to offer yet?"

Pedro's grin went from ear to ear. "Oh, hell yeah."

Tomas's grin was not so wide. "Well, half of the world has seen it."

Carlos looked at him. "We'll make Papa come around if he has a problem."

The grin left Tomas's face. "He *will* have a problem, though."

"But he'll get over it," Pedro added. "We'll make him."

Hours later, during a stopover in Barcelona for fuel and food, they were delayed by a series of events. First, they found out Papadopoulos wasn't even in Athens, two, the authorities kept them in a small room at the airport until Payday sorted the legal side of things out, three, their plane needed repairs, and four, there was a worker's strike at the airport, all delaying them by many hours. But finally, they were back in the air and touched down in Mykonos in the early hours of Monday morning.

"Argh." Carlos arched his back after exiting the plane. "Definitely not enough room for long legs."

Pedro breathed in the air. "God, smell that. Good old Mykonos."

"Right, now, we have our plans. We'll separate once we get past the local cops," Payday said.

"They'll recognise us," Pedro said. "I went to them after Carlos left. They'll know me for sure."

"Then hang at the back of the pack, and hope they don't notice." Payday walked ahead of the team. With six other feds, there were thirteen of them in total, and after a few minutes of to-ing and fro-ing with the local police, Payday waved them all on. They split into three groups; Pedro with Mark and three agents, Tomas with three agents, and Carlos with Tony, Aneeka and Payday. They would take different routes to the Stephanopoulos home, and the agents would stand guard while Payday went inside with the brothers.

Payday checked his watch; 3:30 am. Leading the way, he took directions from Carlos and they all arrived at their parents' house within fifteen minutes.

One of the agents stepped forward and pulled out a lock-picking kit. Since none of the boys had their keys, it was the only way to get inside. Carlos turned the handle and the door slipped quietly open. Seven of them stepped inside and closed the door behind them.

The boys went into their parents' room, and each took a side. Turning the bedside lights on, they covered their parents' mouths. "Shh," they whispered when they woke.

Jenny's eyes grew wide at the sight of her children, and Spiros frowned at the invasion.

"Shhh. Come into the lounge and don't turn the lights on," Carlos whispered. "It's important."

Spiros nodded, and the boys let them up. After grabbing dressing gowns, they turned off the lights and followed them into the lounge.

Payday flicked on a lamp, and Jenny and Spiros saw him, Tony, Aneeka and Mark.

"What's going on?" Spiros demanded.

"Keep your voice down, Mr Stephanopoulos, we don't want your neighbours to know we're here." He flashed his badge. "I'm Special Agent Payday of the FBI, and we need your help."

Jenny was smothering her boys in hugs and kisses.

"Help with what? My boys are home, that's all that matters." She ran her hands through Carlos's hair. "I love it. You look so mature."

"*Our* boys are *criminals*," Spiros spat with venom. "Especially you." He eyed Carlos. "*What* did I teach you?"

"Papa—" Carlos started.

"Mr Stephanopoulos," Payday said sharply, catching Spiros's attention once more. "Your sons *are not* criminals, they have all been set up by Stefano Papadopoulos, and we want to know why." He saw Spiro's eyes widen at the name and Jenny stopped fondling the boys. "Who is he to *you*, Mr Stephanopoulos? And why does he want to set your sons up for crimes they did not commit?"

*****

It was four in the morning in Athens, and Marta Effidopolous sucked Gustoff Dropopolous's cock. Before he came, he spun her around and took her from behind as she held onto the bed sheets, half standing, half kneeling.

He thrust, and it was over within thirty seconds. Letting her go he pushed her to the bed, eyeing her as he zipped up his pants and she rolled onto her back, spreading her legs.

"Need more?"

He eyed off the tits and open pussy, and his tongue went to work.

*****

Spiros stared at Payday. "What do you mean, he set my sons up?"

"Exactly that," Payday replied and told him of the links to Papadopoulos. "Your sons are innocent of every charge against them. They have committed *no* crimes, Mr Stephanopoulos. Now, your son Carlos remembered an incident from when he was seventeen. He was working in the meat shop when Papadopoulos visited. Do *you* remember?" He watched the play of emotions cross Spiro's face.

Spiros glanced from Payday to Carlos and back before he finally spoke. "Stay away from Papadopoulos. He's dangerous."

"But *why* does he have it in for your sons?" Payday asked.

Spiros warily eyed his visitors. He hadn't seen, or heard from Stefano Papadopoulos since that day over seven years earlier. "Just leave it."

"We can't, Papa." Carlos went to his father's side. "This man has set us all up. He set *me* up for rape and murder. His stepson, Andros Poulos, tried to kill Pedro, and *his* illegitimate son kidnapped Tomas after poisoning him—"

"Oh, my God, what?" Jenny cried, one hand flying to her mouth, the other to Tomas. "Spiros," she pleaded.

Carlos glanced from her to his father knowing something was up. He went on. "All of the people involved in this are connected to Stefano Papadopoulos. *Who* is he and *why* would he be doing this? To *you*, to *us?* What did *we* ever do to him?"

They all waited with bated breath.

Spiros looked at his wife's distraught face, sighed, and finally said, "You were born."

*****

In Athens, Stefano Papadopoulos was walking downstairs to the kitchen. He was hungry and wanted something to eat. And maybe he'd wake up Maria, his maid, to service him while she was making him food. He may be seventy-five, but he could still get it up occasionally, with some work. But that didn't stop him wanting to plant it in a woman, and Maria would do. She was in her fifties, with a brat of a daughter he figured was his, so he would never touch her. The mother would have to do.

He passed the kitchen on his way to Maria's room and heard noises coming from the girl's room. The light came underneath the door, and he quietly slipped over and listened.

"Ugh, Gustoff, you are good," Marta said. "You know what to do with your tongue."

Stefano opened the door quietly and peered through the gap. Marta lying naked, sideways, and spread-eagled on her bed with Gustoff, his bodyguard, between her legs. He arched a brow and licked his lips, feeling the stirring in his groin.

"When we tell people we got married?" she asked, wincing at the pain of having her insides sucked out.

He stopped. "What?"

She put her head up and looked down at his face hovering above her bushy thatch. "When we tell everyone we got married? I told you if you helped get rid of Consuela I would marry you and make you heir to Papadopoulos fortune and that happened. He's seventy-five; he's not going to last much longer."

Stefano stood to attention. *What was that about Consuela?*

Gustoff stood up. "I think we should not tell anyone. I think we should keep it a secret."

Marta sat up. "What do you mean you want to keep it a secret? What am I giving it away for? You said you were all for it?"

"I changed my mind." He buttoned his shirt. "That mess was enough. I can't believe I let you get me into that mess."

"You got what you wanted," Marta spat. "Fucking me."

"Yes, and at the time I had no problem shooting Consuela and blowing that Carlos kid all for your daddy's fortune. The fortune you don't even know you'll get," Gustoff said. "You're just the bastard child. He either doesn't know about you, or he denies you exist. You will get nothing. Look at you, shut your legs, you're just a whore."

"You didn't have a problem the night we killed Consuela. You fucked me senseless." Marta's eyes shot daggers at him. "I'll inherit everything, and I'll make sure of it."

"Is that so?" Stefano stepped through the door brandishing the revolver he always carried in his dressing gown pocket. He closed the door behind him to block out any noise. Not that it mattered as he had a silencer on it. "*You* killed my fiancée? *You* killed Consuela? You told me that Carlos Stephanopoulos had killed her, but it was *you*?"

Marta and Gustoff backed up against the bedhead. "No, no, we didn't," they pleaded. "It really *was* him," Marta cried. "He was raping her; we stopped him."

"Stopped him?" Stefano said. "*You're* the ones who involved him in the first place. *You're* the ones who killed her. *You're* the ones who took her from the protection of this house to Mykonos to be corrupted by your vile, wicked ways. Just look at the two of you. Both whores and you made my Consuela a whore too."

"No, no, we didn't," they pleaded.

Stefano fired bullets into their stomachs. "Yes, you did. And you made me believe another person was responsible. Just as well I found out that he wasn't. Oh, yes, I've been sitting on that all these months." He watched their painful, but surprised expressions as they lay dying. "Do you know what the hilarious part of all of this is...?" He waited as they pleaded with their pain-filled eyes. "You're actually brother and sister."

*****

"There's someone I need to talk to," Spiros said. "All of you need to leave while I make the call."

"If it has anything to do with Pap—" Payday was cut off.

"It does, but it *must* remain private," Spiros said and waved everyone out. "It must be private." They all went and sat on the balcony to watch the sky lighten for the new day, and a half hour later, Spiros came back out. "It is done."

"What is?" Payday asked, getting to his feet.

"Papa?" Carlos said, standing. "What's going on?"

Spiros took a moment. "We're going to Athens to see Papadopoulos."

"I can't let you do that." Payday put up a hand in protest.

"You can't stop me," Spiros told him defiantly. "This is something that has to be done. I'll get dressed. We'll leave on the ferry." He escorted Jenny into their room to get dressed.

"What the hell's going on?" Pedro demanded of Carlos as they stood beside Tomas at the railing.

Carlos shook his head and glanced at his brothers. "I have no idea, but I think we're about to find out."

*****

In Athens, Stefano quietly called for his henchmen to remove the bodies of Marta and Gustoff. They were of no consequence to him and would not be needed. He closed and locked the door once the bed had been removed and all belongings were taken. The room was empty once more. He went down the hall and entered Maria's room, removed his robe, laid it over the chair beside the bed and climbed in beside her.

She startled, but calmed when she saw it was him

and lifted her nightgown to accommodate his needs.

All of them.

*****

In Mykonos, Jenny pulled her boys aside for last kisses and hugs. She hadn't seen them in months, and there was no way she was letting them go again without getting her fair share.

"I love you," she told Carlos and squeezed him tight. "As the oldest, you need to look after your brothers. Promise me that."

"I will, Mama," he said, hugging her back fiercely.

"Now, Aneeka told me of the change in plans and that you've all invited some people to come. Who's coming for you?" She pulled back and glanced up at her son. "Someone special I hope."

He smiled. "Very special, Mama."

"Good." She stroked his cheek and moved on to Pedro. "My baby," she murmured, getting a kiss before he grabbed her in a bear hug. "You shouldn't be involved in stuff like this. You're way too young."

"I know, but I'm not a boy anymore, Mama."

"You are to me." She kissed his cheek and pulled back. "You'll always be my baby."

"Mama." He blushed. "I'm twenty now."

"Doesn't matter, you're not an adult yet, so you're still my baby. Always have been, always will be." She moved on to Tomas. "Are you okay?" She took his face into her hands. "You've been so sick and don't look that good."

"I'm getting there," he said, hugging her tightly.

"Do you have anyone special coming?" she asked for only him to hear.

He pulled his head back to look at her and smiled softly. "Yes."

"So, you've found someone?" Her heart soared.

"Yes."

"Is he good to you?"

Tomas's smile broadened. "Very."

"Good." Still hugging him, she looked at her other sons. "Now, you two, I expect you to look after him because he's been so sick *and* because he's your brother and it's what the three of you do. He needs love and care."

"Yes, Mama," they said.

"Good. Now make me proud."

Tomas bent down for another hug, and she kissed him on the head.

Aneeka stayed behind with Jenny as they would meet the men later in Athens. Spiros, the boys, Tony, Mark and the FBI went to the airport to take the plane as it would be faster than the ferry Spiros had suggested. They made sure it was fuelled, climbed aboard, and took off with Tony behind the stick and Mark as co-captain. The trip would take them about thirty minutes.

*****

In Athens, Stefano delighted in all the pleasures that was Maria Effidopolous. His loyal servant for thirty years, taking care of his house, his needs and his sexual appetite, she served in all ways, every way, to please her master. And please him she did. Just a pity she had to fall pregnant and have a bitch of a bastard child.

He came and slowly rocked to a stop, then with a groan of satisfaction rolled off her. "Ugh. Good, as always."

"Is there anything else you need?" She laid a hand on his chest.

He smiled. "No, no, that will be all." He stood, donned his robe, pulled out his gun and fired one shot into her stunned face.

Blood spattered everywhere.

"Well, that is that." He called to his henchmen to clear up the mess. "Help is so hard to find these days. Maybe I'll get a lovely young girl to come work for me."

*****

It was seven o'clock when they flew into Athens and landed at the airport. After hiring cars, they drove to the most expensive part of town and up the driveway of Stefano Papadopoulos's home.

His house was a luxurious one, what one would consider a mansion. Perched high above the city it spanned fifty acres of lush greenery and had twenty-five rooms and a garage big enough for a fleet of cars.

They alighted and slowly made their way to the door.

*****

Aneeka and Jenny made their way to the *Elegance Hotel* that morning and booked in, ordering champagne, drinks and food to be delivered.

"Oh, this is lovely," Jenny said, casting a glance at the rich, luxurious décor of the lobby. "We hardly ever come to Athens. There's no real need to."

"That seems like such a pity," Aneeka told her. "The city is beautiful. I've been here several times in the last few years for photo shoots. I always make time to play tourist and see the sites."

"Oh, yes, we've done the tourist things too, bringing the boys here when they were younger so they could learn about their heritage." They stepped into the lift and went up to their suite. "Spiros wanted them to learn about his half too."

"Of course he would. It's a part of them. Especially Tomas. He looks very much like his father."

"Yes," Jenny told her as they entered their suite. "He does take after his father in looks, but Carlos always intrigued people the most since he doesn't look Greek."

"Yes." Aneeka put her brand-new handbag on the sofa. "That seems to be the thing that people mention most. The fact he looks nothing like a Greek."

Jenny laughed. "Yes. He's gotten that his whole life, poor thing."

After freshening up and settling in, Aneeka called Harry's room to let them know they were there, and shortly after, Harry, Harriet, Connie and Vivian entered the suite.

"Jenny, this is Harry and Harriet DeVille, Connie DeLuca and Vivian Villiers." Aneeka introduced them as they came through the door. "Everyone, this is Jenny Stephanopoulos, Carlos's mother."

They all shook hands, and Jenny asked, "Which one of you got my son into porn?"

Viv and Connie flushed at their parts in it, but Harry guffawed. "Well, I'd like to think that he got *himself* into it. After his sexual endeavours on Mykonos, I'd say the boy was ripe for the picking."

Jenny arched a brow and narrowed her eyes. "I know my son, all three of my sons, have healthy sexual appetites, but that doesn't mean they're ripe for the picking by old fart Lotharios like you to be used for making money by getting their clothes off on the big screen." She lifted her chin in defiance. "I don't approve of what you've done with him, or what he does via his own choices when it comes to working, but I *will not* have you take advantage of my son. *Do you understand me?*" Her tone hardened as she eyed off the man before her. She moved her glance to Harriet. "Or you."

Harry lowered his cigar and stared at Jenny, open mouthed. In all of his years as a porn producer, he had never come across a parent. And he was feeling the bite on his ass from the sass of the fiery Australian woman in front of him. He now knew where Carlos got it from.

Harriet quaked in her boots. As a woman of older years, she had always, at least for the last couple of decades, seen herself as a motherly figure to the boys they hawked. But now that she was up against a mother, the *real* mother of one of her boys, she was feeling highly inadequate.

"You will *not* take advantage of my boy, *do you understand me?*" Jenny looked from one to the other, waiting for their replies.

Harry and Harriet glanced at each other before replying, knowing it was the only thing to do. "Yes, ma'am."

"Good. Now go and sit in the corner and say nothing until you're spoken to," Jenny told them. "You *are not* the important ones here, my boys are." They skulked away, and Connie followed, smirking at the dressing down she had just seen.

Vivian jumped in nervously, wanting to know about Carlos. "How is he? I haven't spoken to him since before the kidnapping and I'm so worried."

Aneeka stopped grinning at the two Harries' discomfort due to the smart as a whip Jenny Stephanopoulos to quickly fill her in without going into detail. "He's fine. They are off doing their man thing and will be back later. You'll see him then."

Viv sighed and held her clutch purse in front of her. "That's good. I can't wait to see him. To tell him I love him and want to spend the rest of my life with him."

That surprised Jenny. That her twenty-four year old son was having a relationship with the forty-year-old model, Vivian Villiers. "Am I to understand you and my son are a couple?"

Viv blushed. "Ah, um, sort of. We, ah, need to talk about it, but we have seen each other since he left Mykonos and I do love him." She waited breathlessly for Jenny to stop staring with her eagle eye. *She'll be okay with it, won't she? I do love her son, that's the only thing that should matter. Oh, God, how I love him so.*

Jenny narrowed her eyes and homed in, holding out an arm in the direction of the bedroom. "*Ms Villiers,* let's have a chat." She led her into the room and motioned for her to sit on the bed.

Vivian gracefully tucked her dress under her and sat, making sure to keep her clutch in front of her stomach. She didn't want anyone knowing until she told Carlos. She looked up at Jenny who stood pacing in front of her.

"Ms Villiers," Jenny started.

"Please, call me Viv," she jumped in.

Jenny arched a brow at the interruption. "Ms Villiers," she said icily. "Am I to understand that you met my son on Mykonos before this trouble began?"

Viv shrank back at the death stare coming from her potential in-law. "Um, yes," she said. "A few days beforehand."

"And were you one of his conquests?" Jenny stopped pacing and stood in front of her, arms crossed. They knew all about Carlos and his women, in fact, she despised it, having not raised him that way. But Spiros had always argued it was the Greek in him and that the boys should bed who they wanted until they got married. Jenny disagreed, glad that they had at least remembered to use protection. She hoped.

"Um," Viv faltered and blushed. "Not quite."

"Then tell me, how did you meet my son?"

Viv took a deep breath. "I had been holidaying on Santorini and came to Mykonos for a while. I was at the bar the day a young blonde girl called him out in front of everyone. I intervened, and she ran off. Carlos went off duty, and I followed him to talk. We…um…" She blushed furiously.

"*Talked…a lot…*apparently," Jenny said. "But then my son did that with *a lot* of females. You're not the first, you know."

"But I hope to be the last," Viv said quickly. "Now, I know I'm older than him, and believe me it's something I've thought about, but the way he makes me feel when we're together it's…" She shrugged lightly. "Magical."

Jenny laughed. "Yes. We've heard that line many, many times. Our Carlos sure knows his stuff in bed. Seems to be a Greek thing according to his father." She sat beside Viv on the bed. "You know you're *far* from being his first? There have been many, *many* women *and girls* before you who all thought Carlos was the one for them."

Viv felt her cheeks burn knowing she was just one of the possible hundreds, if not thousands, of women Carlos had bedded. She looked down at her lap. "I know," finally came out of her mouth. "There was a long line of women before me." She looked at Jenny. "But I'm hoping I'm the last in that line. I know I'm older than him by sixteen years, Mrs Stephanopoulos, but I love him. And I think being with an older woman may settle him down. But that's just my hope."

Jenny examined the woman before her. Gorgeous, slim, and painfully in love with her son. She started feeling inadequate. "Do you think the age difference will be an issue for you? That he may leave you for a younger version of you one day?"

Vivian glanced away as her fingers nervously played with the tassel on her clutch. "I've thought about it. What will he think of me when we hit our tenth, twentieth or thirtieth wedding anniversary? What will he think of me if I grow old and fat and grey?"

"And?"

Viv sighed, shrinking into herself slightly, almost in defeat. "I will hope and pray that you and your husband have raised him well enough to not think that way and to love me until my dying day *regardless* of how I look."

Jenny felt the spark in her chest, and a tear sprang to her eye. "You really love my son *that* much?"

Viv's eyes teared up as she looked at Jenny. "Yes."

*****

Spiros rang the bell and saw Payday take out his badge. "Put that away. We'll have a problem if you don't."

Payday eyed Spiros and saw he was serious. He slipped it back into his pocket and kept on wondering about the relationship between Spiros and Papadopoulos.

A young maid answered the door. "Yes?"

"We need to see Stefano Papadopoulos," Spiros told her.

"Of course." She led them into the entrance, and

they were taken into a spacious room off the back of the house. "May I tell him who's here?"

"Spiros Stephanopoulos."

"Of course." She left, and five minutes later Stefano Papadopoulos came storming into the room.

"How dare you set foot in my house, especially this early in the morning? I've already sacked the maid for letting you in."

"And probably fucked her as well," Spiros muttered under his breath, but his sons heard and eyed him suspiciously.

Stefano stopped when he saw more than just Spiros standing in his lounge room, and the blood drained from his face when he saw the brothers. "You…!" He was deathly white. "You…"

"Yes…us," Carlos said. "Alive and well and in your house."

"No," Papadopoulos muttered and grabbed the back of a chair for support.

Payday moved forward, but Spiros held him back. "Don't speak," he hissed, and in a confused state, Payday stood back.

"We're here to deal with this, Stefano." Spiros stepped toward him. "Why have you set up my sons? What is your deal with them?"

"Sons," Papadopoulos spat, coming back to life. "Half-breeds! That's all they are. Half-breeds that deserve everything they get. And besides, I didn't set them up for anything. That was everyone else's doing. I *saved* them. *I* saved your brat Carlos from murder and rape. *I* saved your brat Pedro from that pathetic, stupid ex-stepson of mine, and *I* saved your brat Tomas from *his* stupid illegitimate brat, Luiz. So don't you stand there and tell me *I've* set them up. Because whatever *they did get, they* deserved."

"And what is it we deserve?" Carlos asked, getting a clear view of the old man with such hatred for them. "We don't *know* you. We've never met you, and until recently we'd never heard of you, or had anything to do with you."

"No." Stefano straightened. "But that stupid stepson of mine was as stupid as his mother was. Thank God she was only my second wife and I got rid of her when I was done with her. As for him, he thought he was a drug kingpin, he did. That had nothing to do with me, but when I found out what he'd done, I did something about it."

"What?" Pedro asked, more confused by the minute. "Why? What did you do to help me? Why would you do *anything* to help me?"

"Because my stupid stepson had plans for you that interfered with the plans *I* had." Stefano's grip tightened on the chair. He could feel the rage inside like a hurricane whirling around. The veins bulged in his neck, and his heart was going faster than it should have been. *All because of Spiros fucking Stephanopoulos and his half-fucking-breed brats. And who the fuck are those other three?*

"And what plans were they?" Pedro asked, feeling tiny cold tendrils of terror rise up through his chest.

"Death," Papadopoulos said.

Pedro's brows made a slight move into a frown

before settling back into their normal position. "Then you may as well have let Andros do the job."

Stefano sneered. "Except I wanted the job of making your lives a misery myself."

"And your fiancée…was *she* collateral damage?" Carlos asked. "Sending one of your goons to do the job and frame me for it?"

Stefano shrugged and felt a little more relaxed. "I cannot claim that. I have only just found out that my maid and her husband took Consuela to Mykonos, and involved you in that with the idea to set you up and make it look as if someone else was at fault and they were not. They have been dealt with."

Payday opened his mouth, but Tony's hand on his arm and a warning look made his mouth close.

"Of course they have been," Spiros said. "So, let's get down to the bottom line, shall we. What do you want with my sons…?"

*****

Angelina flew into Athens with Greta Von Burro and arrived at the hotel. They were taken straight up to Aneeka's room by a bell boy who carried their bags, and there she met her lover's mother.

"Mrs Stephanopoulos, what a pleasure meeting the woman who gave birth to the gorgeous god that is Pedro." Greta held out her hand to shake, but retracted it when she saw Jenny's icy gaze and unmoving hands. She saw Harry and Harriet shrinking back into the corner and wondered what was going on.

"Ms Von Burro," Jenny spat. "The woman who turned my baby boy into a sex machine for the world to see. Definitely *not* nice to meet you."

"Uh," Greta mumbled. "Well…" She wiped the sweat from her palms in pretence of smoothing her skirt. She'd never met a parent either, but after seeing Harry in the corner, she realised she was in for a grilling.

"*What possessed you* to ask my baby to do pornos for you?" Jenny asked, staring her down. "*He's twenty for Christ's sake,* barely legal in some states, and I'm sure barely legal in America. But no, you had to snatch him from his cradle and make him yours. Yours for the world to see and manipulate and use for your own benefit. Get off on it do you?" Jenny moved closer. "Get off on seeing him naked, did you? Want him for yourself? Hoped that you could take him for a ride like the DeVilles wanted to take Carlos?" She waved an arm at the shrinking Harries in the corner. "You disgust me," she went on. "Don't *ever* think that I will be happy with what you've done. Don't *ever* think that I will support it because I won't. I will *never* support porn let alone my sons being in it. *Do I make myself clear?*" She waited for the stunned expression to slide from Greta's icy Swedish face.

Greta gulped. Never had she been reamed out before for anything because no one ever went up against the iciness of Greta Von Burro. And so never had she ever been reamed out for being a porn producer, but then she had never come across a woman as fierce as the one before her.

"Well?" Jenny demanded.

"Um, yes, um, Mrs Stephanopoulos, very clear."

"Good, now go and sit in the corner with your cohorts." She sent Greta scurrying to the corner with her tail between her legs, as she had Harry, and turned her attention to the very young girl with her left arm in a sling. The girl looked frightened. Having backed up at the attack, she had nearly fallen over the suitcase and cabin bag she'd brought with her. "You must be Angelina Poulos?"

"Um, yes Mrs Stephanopoulos," Angelina nervously breathed, taking a small step forward. "I wasn't sure if I'd meet you here...or not..." She quickly wiped her hand on her pants before shaking hands with Jenny.

"And you're dating Pedro?" Jenny said, holding on.

"Um, oh, ah, yes," Angelina said. "We, uh, met at the club he worked at and started dating, and then he came to New York with me."

Jenny examined the girl's face. Nervous, young, but old enough for Pedro? She tilted her head. "And what do you do?"

Angelina blinked slowly, her brain working even slower. "Ah...I'm a student at Juilliard...in New York."

Jenny relaxed. "Oh, you're a musician, how wonderful. With Pedro being a DJ you both have that in common. Tell me about the last few months." She led Angelina to the bedroom and started the grilling she'd already put Vivian through.

"Tell me, what do you think of my son?"

Angelina sat on the bed and smiled. "I love him."

"Why?"

"What?" Angelina became momentarily confused.

Jenny smiled at the girl, who was younger than her baby. "*Why* do you love him?"

Angelina smiled, relaxed by the question. "Because he's amazing. He's gentle and kind and caring, and he loves me for me and not who I am..." She glanced away. "Was."

"Yes, I heard about your father. I'm sorry."

Angelina glanced out the window as tears came to her eyes. "I'm not sure I am."

"Understandable," Jenny said. "But what does that mean for you and my son?"

Angelina wiped her eyes. "I don't know what you mean?"

"Do you expect him to take care of you? Will you continue at school? What will you do now your father's dead?"

Angelina shook her head. "I hope to continue school, and I have no idea what I'm going to do now my father's dead. I suppose I should talk to our lawyer while I'm here in Greece."

"But what for you and Pedro? What sort of life will you have, do you want?" Jenny studied the girl beside her. She was way too young to deal with the issues that were going on. Especially the ones concerning her father.

"I don't know, Mrs Stephanopoulos." Angelina looked at her. "All I know is I love him and that he is my forever."

*****

In the lounge room, Greta sat next to Harry on the sofa. "What the fuck was that all about?"

Harry looked at her. "You're kidding, right?" When she shook her head, he continued. "That was a mother who is pissed off at us making her babies take their clothes off and fuck for a living."

"But that…she…" Greta took a breath. "I have never come across a parent before. That was *not* something I want to do again."

"Then don't get on a mother's bad side," Harriet said. "Why do you think we avoid parents at all cost?"

"But this time it couldn't be helped," Harry said, puffing on his cigar. "Carlos started off with trouble and has ended with trouble. And to sort it all out, we had to come here."

"And now we've met the parents," Harriet said.

"Oh, no," Connie said from her position on a couch. "You haven't met *Spiros* Stephanopoulos yet."

*****

Stefano shrugged again. "To kill them."

"Of course," Spiros said again. "You want them out of the family."

The others turned to stare at him.

"What else?" Papadopoulos asked. "We can't have half-breeds taking over the family business."

"Except they wouldn't be," Spiros barked. "When I moved to Australia I was disowned. I only moved back when my father died."

"Yes, except I can't be sure of that," Papadopoulos

said. "The old man hasn't said who'll take over the business and except for you, I'm the only one left."

"Doesn't mean he'll leave it to you," Spiros told him. "He could get rid of it completely and leave it to neither of us."

"Wait," Carlos interrupted, holding his hand up. "The two of you are related?"

Papadopoulos chuckled. "You haven't told them?"

"Have you?" Spiros snapped back. With a deep sigh, he glanced at his sons. "Stefano is your grandfather's brother-in-law."

"So our great-uncle-in-law," Pedro slowly worked out.

"Yes, by marriage," Papadopoulos said. "Smart, for a half-breed." He scored a filthy look from Pedro in return. Not that he cared.

"So what the hell is going on? What has your relationship with our father got to do with us?" Carlos asked.

"He doesn't want you taking over the family business when his father-in-law dies. He's not blood, but you boys are. And it gets handed down to his blood relatives, not in-laws," Spiros said.

Carlos was confused. "We don't want the family business. We have our own lives, and money, and jobs."

"As fuckers on the big screen with ten inch cocks. Hardly a job," Papadopoulos scoffed.

"What even *is* the family business?" Pedro asked, just as confused as everyone else besides his father and great uncle.

"You name it they do it," Spiros said. "Sex, drugs,

prostitutes, counterfeit shit. Anything and everything. Guns…money…"

"Definitely not something we want to be involved with," Carlos said.

"Not the way it works in this family," Papadopoulos spat. "When the old man dies it will go to your father, then you."

"Giorgio knows I don't want it." Spiros scowled.

"Then it goes to your half-breeds, and that's why I wanted the luxury of killing them myself. So they don't get to inherit. It belongs to me and me alone." Stefano whipped out the gun from his smoking jacket pocket.

Payday, Tony and Mark whipped out theirs and stood in front of Spiros and the boys.

"Ah," Stefano said. "I wondered who you three were. Armed guards? Assassins? Bodyguards? Undercover Feds?" He shrugged. "Doesn't matter, I have my own. Get them," he yelled at the doorway.

But no one came in except for one bulked-up muscle man in a blue suit wheeling a shrivelled up old man in a wheelchair.

*****

Roger finally arrived in Athens with Marcus and Violet Seralift, Bette Olander, Bertha St John and Willow Bertran, and went straight to the hotel. He was greeted by Aneeka and Jenny, who Tomas had told him all about. Glancing around, he saw people he knew of, but had never met. Once the introductions with Jenny were made, Marcus and Violet were given the severe tongue lashing from her about getting her child into the porn industry.

"Who in God's name do you think you all are?" she asked them, turning her head to include the two Harries and Greta in her question. "Who in the hell gave you permission to make children do naked movies?"

"They're not children, and it's not like they didn't make a choice," Marcus started before Jenny cut him off with her icy glare.

"Oh, I know they made a choice, especially Carlos and Pedro, but Tomas is different," she said. "He's quiet and an introvert; this is *not* something he would have gone into willingly."

"Well, he was certainly willing to fuck my fiancé," Bertha muttered from her recently acquired spot on the sofa.

"What did you say?" Jenny's glare turned on her and Bertha withered into her seat. *"I know all about your fiancé,"* she spat with a pointed finger. "The arsehole who took advantage of my son while *engaged to you.* That made him absolutely gut wrenchingly sick, so don't you *ever* bring it up again, *especially* in front of my face." She turned back to Marcus. "So high and mighty with your fancy clothes and fancy homes all paid for by men and women taking their clothes off and baring all for the world to see. You should be so ashamed and disgusted with yourselves, but *clearly* none of you are. Have you *ever* thought about the families of these boys? What *they* think, what *they* feel, what *they* want? Or is it all about the exploitative

means of making a quick buck from young and naïve boys and girls who don't know any better, who are taken with all the glitz and glamour of being in a movie. *Regardless* of what it is?"

She turned her back to them with a huff and crossed her arms. "Go and sit in the corner with *them* and keep your mouths shut. You may be my son's bosses, but that doesn't give you the right to waltz in here and expect open arms and a welcoming hug." They quickly moved to the corner with the others, mouths open, yet stunned into silence.

And all had quaked in their shoes having never dealt with a parent before.

Jenny heaved for air a few times, her heart pounding with the adrenaline. Sighing, she turned her head to Roger who was also quaking after her diatribe. "Do you love my son?" she asked quietly. Searching his face, she saw pure joy and happiness flood over it when he talked about Tomas.

"Yes. Oh, yes. I love him, Mrs Stephanopoulos. I've never felt this way about anyone, and Tomas is it for me." He felt weak at the knees just talking about his lover, but his stomach was clenched in knots at what was about to happen.

Jenny breathed and smiled. "Good, now come this way." She led him into the bedroom and motioned for him to sit. "Tell me, how did you meet?"

"Uh." He sat on the bed. "At a club one night. He was dancing with Willow Bertran when he caught my eye. I went over to the bar and chatted to him. He was…" A smile crept over his lips. "Mesmerising."

Jenny took note of the smile. "So, it started from there?"

"Yes. He then came to the studios with Bette to have a look at what happens in movie making, and I ran into him, surprised that he was there. He was scared of what was going on because we were… well… we were filming a steam room scene."

"Ah," Jenny said. "That would *not* have helped him."

"No, you're right, it didn't. He bolted, and I followed. I knew something was going on and got it out of him by talking. He opened up, and the grief eased. We started hanging out and then…things happened."

Jenny smiled at his happiness then brought up *that* subject. "You know about Luiz?"

The smile disappeared. "Yes. Do you know what Luiz did?"

Murderous anger washed over her face. "Yes. And I'm glad the bastard is dead."

"So am I."

"I'm sure you are. I heard you'd been arrested for the murders. How are you holding up?" She took in his features as he spoke.

He nodded briefly. "Okay. Glad I've been freed and will be reunited with Tomas."

Jenny gave him the once over. "I hear your Australian accent. Where from?"

Roger was mildly surprised. "Wollongong. Did Tomas tell you?"

She shook her head. "I only got the bullet points of what's happened."

"Well, I've been in America for two years. Decided

to try my luck at the movies."

"And that's how you got into pornos?"

"Ah." He laughed lightly and wiped his palms on his jeans. "I was auditioning for normal movies and somehow found my way to Marcus Seralift who offered me a job. I was having sex with girls in them for a while…but knew I couldn't continue."

"Because you're gay?"

He looked her square in the eye. "Yes."

"How long?"

"Mmm," he blinked, "close to ten years I think."

"So, you would have helped Tomas deal with his sexuality then?"

Roger nodded slightly. "Yes…when we met he was clearly still traumatised from Luiz, but we talked a bit, and he wanted to love and be loved regardless of which sex it was with. It just happened that he chose a man to be with."

She nodded, and a soft smile came to her lips. "Thank you for that. I wasn't sure if I'd be able to help him. And his father certainly wouldn't have."

Roger watched her. "Will he have a problem with it now? If he does, it could hurt Tomas more than anything."

"Not if I can help it," she said. "No one hurts my babies. Not even my husband." She tilted her head. "Are you safe? Do you use protection?"

"Always, every time, even in the movies."

"Good. I want my baby safe. Did you get him into pornos?"

He blinked slowly and sighed. "I'm not sure."

"What do you mean?"

"Well, the ladies that arrived today knew Violet and took him to the club where we met. Bette then brought him to the studios and he met Marcus. Next thing, he and I are talking about making movies because he wanted to know the ins and outs and how I could do it." He looked down, feeling a bit embarrassed. "I asked him if he'd ever thought of making a movie with a lover, and one night at the studio after I'd filmed one, we re-enacted the steam room scene. I wanted to make the memories happy ones so he wasn't affected by Luiz anymore. It worked on that part, but Marcus and Violet saw us and wanted Tomas to join the company."

"He obviously did."

He looked up at her. "Yes, but not right away. He put some serious thought into whether he could do it or not, and he decided to do it so we could spend more time together. For us, it's not about the movies; it's about being intimate every day. The closeness, the moments we're together, the cameras are forgotten, and sometimes the crew walks out and just leaves us alone to do our thing. It's not about the *making* of a movie; it's about spending as much time together as possible. It's about the time we spend making love and being intimate. It's about me loving him and him loving me. When we're together, in that moment, it's the most beautiful, peaceful moment ever and we never want it to stop. That's why we do it, to spend as much time together as possible."

"That's how you feel about my son?"

The smile came back, flying across his face until it

was ear to ear. "Yes. I love him *so much*, Mrs Stephanopoulos. He is the man I want to spend the rest of my life with."

*****

In the suite, Marcus and Violet were reservedly greeting everyone else. "Harry." Marcus shook hands with him after Harry had stood. "What in blazes was that?"

Harry guffawed. "We were just talking about that. Her babies are *not* to be messed with."

"Well, fuck me," Marcus said. "I thought we were here to support her sons, but it looks like Mama Bear has her claws out."

"I wouldn't be too smarmy if I were you," Greta told him. "She reamed us all out."

"And here I was thinking I was too old and too done with bullshit." Marcus sat beside Violet on the sofa.

"Not to be told off by a parent you're not," Violet told him. "I wonder what she's saying to Roger?"

Harry turned to Viv. "What did she do to you?"

Viv came out of her dream world. "Mmm? She asked me about my relationship with Carlos and whether I loved him."

"Is that all?" Connie asked. "I'm surprised she didn't pick me off. After all, I had him before you."

Viv wearily looked at her. "Don't remind me."

Greta glanced at Angelina who was shrinking into her spot on the sofa, looking fragile and tiny. "What about you? What did she say to you?"

Angelina lifted her head. "Pretty much the same

thing. I get it. From the way Pedro talks about his family, they're all really close. His mother was bound to defend her babies."

"Except they're not babies anymore," Marcus said. "They're full grown men who can look after themselves."

"Can they?" Harry asked. "Look at all the trouble they've gotten themselves into. Even before we took them on."

"And can you believe we all took on a Stephanopoulos brother?" Marcus added. "Imagine the money we're going to make when we advertise the shit out of that detail."

Greta arched a brow. "Pedro did mention another brother to us. Clearly, that is Tomas, and we had come up with the idea of maybe getting all three into a movie at some stage. What do you think of that?"

Marcus and Harry both looked at her. "Have you *seen* Tomas?" Marcus asked.

"In a picture," Greta said. "So I can't wait to see him in real life."

"You know he's gay, right?" Marcus added.

"When you have three incredibly hot brothers with massive cocks in a porn movie getting naked and fucking other people, what's it going to matter?" Greta said.

*****

"Stefano," the old man said, and Papadopoulos spun around.

His eyes widened. "Giorgio I…wasn't…expecting you. What are you doing here?" He smoothed his jacket, but still held onto his gun.

"Put it away, Stefano." Giorgio waved a withered old hand as he moved into the room. "Spiros."

"Giorgio." Spiros wearily eyed the scene before them.

"Gentleman. Put your guns away." He looked at Payday, Tony and Mark. "There is no one else coming in. My men took care of your men, Stefano. So we shall wrap this up fairly quickly," Giorgio said before spying the boys. He blinked in wonderment. "My great-grandsons. Let me see you."

The boys looked to their father who gave a stiff nod, and they stood around him.

"Ah, Tomas, you look just like my son, Giorgio, when he was young. Pedro, you have the mix. Your grandfather and father's head of hair and jaw, and your mother's eyes. And Carlos, you look like Jenny. How is she, Spiros?"

"Fine," he muttered. "With no thanks to what Stefano has been putting this family through."

"Yes, yes, so you told me, which is why I've come to pay him a visit."

Stefano glanced from Giorgio to Spiros. "What you told him? And just what *have* you told him?"

"Everything," Spiros replied.

"And now I'm here," Giorgio said. "Paying you a little visit to straighten things out."

Stefano preened a little. "Well, you haven't done that before. I'm honoured."

"Don't be," Giorgio said. "I won't tolerate my boys being set up for murder, especially by my hateful bastard of a son-in-law."

"But I—"

"Don't interrupt," the old man thundered. "I always hated you. The way you married into the family and used my daughter for your own benefits. What you did was appalling."

"What do you mean *what I did*?"

"You killed her," Giorgio bellowed.

"Now, just a minute," Stefano said. "I did not."

"You drove her to it with your philandering ways because you couldn't keep your cock in your pants."

"I never—"

"Yes, you did, stop denying it," Giorgio rasped, coughing and spluttering. "You cheated and clawed your way to the top, and when she couldn't give you the child you desperately wanted to continue the bloodline, she died of a broken heart. And then you got stuck with Andros's mother. What was her name? Caterina? You got rid of her soon enough, and Consuela went the same way."

"I had nothing to do with that." Stefano put a hand up in defence. "Nothing."

"Maybe not, but that bastard child with your housekeeper did."

Stefano nodded. "And I've taken care of that."

"I bet you have. Just like you took care of my Giorgio. My son."

Spiros's eyes narrowed at that little tidbit of news. "You! You had something to do with my father's death?"

"Ah…well…" Stefano smoothed his hair. "As much as I'd like to take credit for that…ahhhh…" He fell to his knees, blood seeping from his right knee cap.

"What the bloody hell did you do that for?" he screamed and grabbed his leg.

Giorgio shot him in the shoulder, the gun hidden by the blanket across his knees.

Payday went for Stefano's gun and kicked it out the way.

"Stay back," Spiros warned him. "Don't get involved with this. The less you know or do, the better."

Payday nodded, but kept his gun handy.

"What have you done?" Stefano screamed, bleeding all over the expensive ten thousand dollar rug he was lying on.

"What I should have done a long time ago," Giorgio said and raised the gun. "For my Giorgio, for my Marishka, and now, for my great-grandsons." He fired one last bullet. It landed between the eyes of Stefano Papadopoulos.

Silence.

No one would miss Stefano Papadopoulos. He had no children, he had no wives. All he had was his mansion, his businesses, and his money. The mansion and the money would now go to his next of kin. No, no one would miss Stefano Papadopoulos.

"Giorgio," Spiros finally said, eying his grandfather.

"Go, go," the old man replied wearily, dropping the gun into his lap. He was tired, and knew it was almost time. He had waited all of his last decades to deal with Stefano and should have way back then, but had left it until it was almost too late. He gazed up into the faces of his grandson and great-grandsons. "We'll clean up the mess. Go, go."

Spiros urged the boys toward the door, and Giorgio grasped his hand weakly as he passed. He pulled him down to whisper in his ear. Spiros nodded and followed the others out the door.

*****

All seven of them entered the suite half an hour later, in a morose, sombre state.

Jenny was waiting and gave her boys a hug and a kiss as each came through the door. Tony, Mark and Payday stood to the side of the room, but Spiros stayed beside her, casting a wary eye over the people surrounding them.

Carlos spied Viv over his mother's shoulder. "Viv." He ran to her, swept her into his arms and spun around. "Oh, Viv." He held her tight. "You're here."

"I'm here." She laughed. "Of course I'm here." They kissed and walked over to the side of the suite for a quiet moment.

"Angie!" Pedro took Angelina in his arms and carried her tiny frame to the other side of the room away from prying eyes. "God, I missed you." His lips found hers, and the passion stirred.

She pulled away and blushed. "Your parents are here," she whispered.

"So," he whispered back and grinned.

"Roger!" Tomas rushed over to him and hugged him. "I'm so glad you're here."

Spiros saw it and frowned. "Do *not* tell me my son is—"

"There is nothing wrong with that, and *you will not* have a problem with it," Jenny said forcefully in his ear.

"But he is a Greek—"

"He's also Australian!"

"Ugh." Spiros gave in with a defeated bow of his head.

Carlos and Pedro curiously eyed the man who had stolen their brother's heart, but kept to themselves, lost in their own moments with their other halves.

"Mr Stephanopoulos." Harry, Harriet, Greta, Marcus and Violet moved up to them. "Pleasure to meet you, fine young men you have there. Fine young men indeed."

Spiros eyed all five and knew exactly who they were and what his wife had done to them. "I know," he said. "Yet look what you've done to them. Put them naked on the big screen."

"Yes, well," Harry harrumphed, glancing at his wife, Marcus, Violet and Greta. "We only show what God *and his parents* gave him." He slapped Spiros on the arm and got a stony look in return. His hand retreated, and they skulked back to their corner.

"You did a number on them, didn't you?" he asked his wife as he continued to eye them off, skulking in the corner of the suite.

"You better bloody believe it!" The Australian came out in her.

"Good!"

"That went well," Violet said sarcastically walking beside Harriet.

"What did you expect?" Harriet replied. "A thank

you?" They sat back on their sofa.

"No, but do you see how gorgeous the boys all are. We *need* to do a movie with all three of them." Greta eyed off Tomas's dark features.

"Mmm," Marcus murmured, seeing all three in the flesh. "You may be right, Greta, you may be right."

Thinking about the mega bucks they would bring in, Harry nodded in agreement.

Jenny stood watching her family. The boys were back home, they had partners, and were happy. They had jobs which clearly made *them* happy, but not her. She frowned. Not one bit did she like seeing her babies on the big screen completely naked and having sex for all to see. Not one bit at all. She slid her arm through Spiros's, and her life with him flashed back twenty-five plus years to when they met, married, had Carlos, then Tomas, then Pedro. Moving from Australia to Greece and all of the problems it involved. "Has it been sorted?" she asked.

Spiros nodded. "It certainly has."

"Forever?"

Spiros looked at her. "Until Giorgio dies and then we probably start again."

She sighed. "Let's hope that ends today too."

"Let's," Spiros replied and watched his young, handsome sons with their lovers. "How can they have partners when they do what they do to other people?"

"I have no idea," Jenny said. "Except in Tomas's case, he works *with* his partner, so I guess that makes it easier."

Spiros sighed and shook his head. "Sex. For the

love of holy God, they had to get involved with sex. Why couldn't they just find nice girls, get married, and settle down?"

Jenny laughed softly. "I think two of them are already on their way to that."

Spiros looked at Tomas in Roger's arms. "You know you won't get grandchildren out of them two."

"I know," she said quietly as she watched them. "But that's okay."

He looked at his wife. "Is it?"

She looked back and took a breath. "It is… Okay, everyone, gather round. We have food and drink, and it's high time you told us all what the hell just happened."

For the next two hours, each Stephanopoulos told his story from start to finish. They recounted the trip to Stefano's and how it ended. Payday retold his story about how he got involved, and when he was done, he bade them all goodbye.

"I'll leave you all to it. There's not a lot I can do now, with Stefano Papadopoulos dead, and the boys out of danger." He shook Spiros's and Jenny's hands. "Good to have met you both, and remember, your sons are not criminals…yet," he joked. "Oh, and you have the suite free of charge until tomorrow, courtesy of the FBI." He waved the room goodbye.

Aneeka, Tony and Mark took that as their cue to leave since they had no passports, or papers, and needed Payday to take them home. They told everyone they would see them back in the States to wrap things up.

After goodbyes all round, Marcus and Violet took Harry, Harriet and Greta to meet Tomas. They couldn't wait to see the Stephanopoulos brother who actually *looked* Greek up close and in person.

"Hello." Tomas removed himself from Roger's arms and shook hands with them.

"Well, hello," Greta purred. "Pedro mentioned a brother, but we didn't dare to hope that you would be as gorgeous as the other two."

Tomas raised an amused brow. "Well, thank you?"

Harry peered closely through his glasses. "Mmm, you look nothing like Carlos, but we could do something with you if we did a threesome. People love Carlos in Hollywood. He's got the beach boy look."

"He does drive the girls wild with his long hair and Adonis looks, but it looks like he's been shorn. Your idea?" Tomas asked, glancing over at his brother's shorter hair style. "We tried getting him to cut it for years, and he never did, so we called him Samson for a while. How'd you manage it?"

Harry laughed. "Not me, young man, it was the running away from authorities and needing a change of look."

Tomas nodded. "He looks better."

"We think so," Harriet said, twirling her pearls.

"Now, let me introduce you to Pedro," Greta said, and they moved on.

Tomas curled up in Roger's arms again and watched the scene unfold with a smile on his face. "This is weird."

"How so?" Roger asked, breathing in the scent of

the love of his life as he nuzzled his face gently.

Tomas responded in turn. "Seeing them eye us like sharks that haven't eaten in weeks. They're up to something. Did you hear the bit about a threesome...?"

"Pedro, this is Marcus and Violet Seralift, Tomas works for them, and Harry and Harriet DeVille, the bosses of Carlos."

"Hey." Pedro shook hands with all four. "So, you're the one who got Carlos into the game and changed his name?" he said to Harry.

"Yep, that's me. I know a good thing when I see one." He tucked his thumbs into his belt and puffed on his cigar. "And I see another one right now."

Pedro smiled. "If you've got your eye on me I'm taken." He slid his arm around Angelina. "Greta's got me for how many more movies?" he asked her.

"Eight at the moment," she said. "They're selling like hot cakes. Is that what you Americans say?"

Marcus eyed him up and down as did Harriet and Violet. "Why do none of you look alike?" he asked.

"That could be a good thing," Violet said. "Especially if we do the movie with all three. Can't have them looking the same. We've already used triplets."

"What's this about a movie?" Pedro asked.

"Don't worry about it, darling," Greta said. "We'll talk later. Now, let me meet Carlos."

Harry led the way over to his prize possession, leaving Pedro and Angelina shaking their heads at the merry little procession. "Carlos, my boy, meet Marcus and Violet Seralift, and Greta Von Burro. Your brothers work for them."

Carlos, annoyed at having his quiet moments with Viv intruded upon, eyed Harry balefully. "Can't we meet another time? I just want to be with Viv."

"After all the trouble we went through with you, you can spare a few minutes." Harry pointed his finger at him.

Carlos shook hands before sliding them around Viv again. "Got my little brother into porn did you?"

"You have *seen* your brother?" Greta asked. "He's not so little."

"And neither is Tomas. The three of you are going to be huge, famous," Marcus said.

Carlos grinned. "We already *are* huge, or hadn't you noticed?"

Jenny had been keeping an ear on the conversations and finally had enough. Walking over to the group she told the producers, "It's time all of you left so the family can have some alone time."

After the trauma she had caused them earlier, they knew not to argue, especially with the determined look on her face now, so Harry, Harriet, Greta, Marcus and Violet bade everyone adieu, much to Jenny's relief. They just had a few left to go before they could get down to the family.

In their own little world, Vivian and Carlos were alone again. He leant on the edge of a cupboard, arms around her while she stroked his face.

"I've done a lot of thinking since you were kidnapped."

"About what?" He smiled up at her beautiful face.

"Us."

"Us?"

She smiled and nuzzled his cheek. "Yes…us… I love you, Carlos, and I've never been loved by, or been so in love with anyone else in my life. And with everything that's happened… I…need to be with you…" She stroked his cheek and gazed deeply into his crystal blue eyes. "Do you feel the same?"

"Yes, of course I want to be with me, too," he joked with a straight face.

She laughed. "Silly. Not what I meant."

"I know," he said. "I want to be with you, too." He gazed into her eyes. "Will you marry me, Viv?"

"What?" That took her by surprise.

"Will you marry me?" he repeated.

"Oh…yes," she whispered against his lips. "Yes." They kissed. "I guess it's a good thing you asked because…" Pausing, she had a secretive little smile on her face. "Because we're going to be a family." Moving his right hand to her stomach, she watched his expression change.

Across the room, Tomas and Roger were gazing up into each other's eyes while Tomas recounted his traumatic experience. Roger held him tightly, not wanting to let go, even for a minute, and Tomas loved him even more for it. "I love you."

Roger smiled. "I love you, too." His lips lightly met his lover's.

"Did Mama have a word with you?" Tomas smoothed Roger's shirt.

"Oh, she certainly did," Roger said. "Also gave a piece

of her mind to Marcus and Violet, and Harry and Greta before them. I think almost everyone had an earful."

"Was she okay with you?" Tomas searched Roger's eyes for the answer.

Roger smiled. "She was fine. *More* than fine. She was angry at what Luiz had done to you, and grateful that you at least had me to confide in about your sexuality."

Tomas returned the smile as his fingers played with Roger's polo collar. "So am I."

Roger glanced up to see Spiros frowning in his direction. "I'm not sure about your father, though."

Tomas breathed deeply, but couldn't bring himself to look. "Let's hope Mama can bring him round. I know my brothers are on my side. That's four against one."

Standing near the window, Pedro and Angelina were having their own moment. "I love you so much Angie and I know we're young, but I love you and never want to be apart from you." His arms held onto her tightly, holding her like a fragile little bird that needed protecting.

She snuggled into his chest as best she could with her arm in a sling. "I love you, too," she whispered. "And there's something you need to know." She looked up into his eyes. "Pedro—"

"Will you marry me, Angie?"

Shock thundered over her face. "What?"

He pulled a small ring box from his pocket and opened it. "Will you marry me?" Staring down into her face he saw every emotion rain down over it, confusing him as to what was going on inside her at that moment.

"Oh," she breathed. "I guess it's a good thing you asked because…" She took a deep breath. "I'm pregnant," she blurted quietly.

Pedro didn't know what to say so all he said was, "What?"

"I'm pregnant," she whispered fiercely. "I took a test when you were missing, and I've thought about it. I'm going to continue at Juilliard until the baby and then do part-time. We can afford a nanny can't we…if you still have your job at 69…?"

Pedro felt emotion after emotion roll through him like ocean waves. "Oh, God, Angie," he gasped. "Oh, God." He kissed her. "I love you, and I want this. Us. Will you marry me?"

"Yes," she said urgently.

He slid the ring carefully onto her finger, completely unaware of what his brother was going through.

Carlos was staring at Viv in shock. "We're having a baby?" The smile left his face, and he looked down at her stomach. "What?"

"We're having a baby," she repeated, worried by his expression.

A noise came from his throat. "Ah, oh, we're having a baby. A baby?"

"Yes," she whispered. "Aren't you happy?"

Emotion after emotion hit him like a ten tonne brick. "Yes…oh…God…yes." He kissed her passionately and then turned to tell everyone, but spied the ring on

Angelina's hand from across the room. "Hey, little brother, where'd you get that ring from? How dare you beat me to it!"

Pedro's head flew up in astonishment, his eyes wide in shock. "What?" His head swivelled around the room and back as he glanced at everyone's faces. "What?"

"I just asked Viv to marry me," Carlos told everyone, "but you beat me to it with a ring." He glanced at Viv. "Sorry, I don't have one yet. I've been kinda busy."

She laughed. "Don't worry, we'll get one. Maybe here in Athens?" she teased.

He smiled and held her tight. "Maybe."

"Wait, wait," Jenny called, holding her hands out towards them. "So, that means *two* of my sons are getting married?" She looked back and forth between Carlos and Pedro, spying Carlos's hand on Vivian's stomach. "And…a baby?" she questioned.

Carlos nodded. "And having a baby over here."

"Ah," Jenny screamed and raced over to them, taking him into her arms in a ferocious motherly hug. "Oh, my God, you're having a baby. Oh, my baby's having a baby." She kissed his cheek before finally letting go, and looking at Viv, she placed a hand on her arm. "Welcome to the family."

"Thank you," Viv said, still feeling the effects of the grilling several hours before.

"And over here too." Pedro waved his hand. He glanced down at Angelina who now wore the small diamond ring on her finger. "Apparently, we're having a baby too."

Jenny stared in astonishment. "What! But…you're both so young." She moved over to them. "A baby is a big deal, and with your parents being dead who will you have to look after you and the baby?" she asked Angelina.

Angelina looked downcast. "I don't know. I guess Pedro will look after me now." She looked up at his Greek hair and Australian blue eyes. "We're a family now."

Jenny saw the look of pure love and adoration in her son's eyes. "Yes," she said softly. "*We* are family now." She took them both into her arms. "Welcome to the family. Your *new* family. You're not alone anymore," she told Angelina who promptly burst into tears. "Aw, there, there." Jenny patted her back and led her into the bedroom with Viv and the other ladies hot on her trail while the men stood around awkwardly not knowing what to do with a crying woman. After giving her a pep talk and freshening up, they came back out, leaving the boys and their partners to acquaint themselves with each other.

"Pedro, Tomas, this is Vivian Villiers, supermodel, and wife and mum-to-be." Carlos smiled broadly as he introduced the love of his life as she stood in his arms.

"Cool." Pedro shook her hand. "You know he had pictures of you on his wall when he was fourteen?"

She laughed. "Yes, he told me the first day we met." Stroking his face, she added, "But how could I *not* love a man who masturbated over me as a teenager."

Surprised guffaws went round the six of them, and Carlos went deep red as he closed his eyes. "Oh, God,

Viv, how could you say that?" he said.

"Because it's probably true." She laughed again.

Carlos tried to get the attention away from him. "And Pedro, introduce us to our new sister-in-law-to-be."

Pedro slipped an arm around Angie's waist. "Angelina Poulos, my brothers Carlos and Tomas. And don't worry, Carlos, she's already seen your cock in action and still prefers mine. After all, I *do have an inch* on you."

"Ouch!" Viv looked at Carlos. "Are you gonna let your *little* brother get away with that? After all, you *did* just win Best Cock of the Year?"

"An award I'm *sure* I'll win next year," Pedro bragged to everyone.

Carlos shook his head in amusement and embarrassment, but refused to play, so he glanced at Tomas and Roger, waiting for Tomas to make introductions. But when he didn't, he spoke up. "I'm Carlos, and that clown is Pedro." He tilted his head in his youngest brother's direction. "And apparently you're Roger." He scanned the tall brunet with the half-Australian accent.

Roger smiled, shy and slightly embarrassed by the small talk. Even though he was gay and worked in porn as well, the way everyone was talking to each other made him feel out of his depth, talk wise.

Tomas came to and blushed. "Mmm? Yeah, ah, this is Roger." He glanced at his lover and got the goofy Stephanopoulos grin on his face as he slid his arm through Roger's and buried his face in his shoulder.

"Good to meet you, Roger." Carlos stuck out his hand to shake, and Pedro followed suit. "You plan on sticking around, or are you going to run out on our brother?"

Tomas's head shot up, and he looked at him in alarm.

But Roger stood his ground. He was coming into a family of strong willed Greek Australian men, and being Australian himself, and having Tomas as his lover, knew he *could* stand his ground. Besides, he had a few inches on all of them. "Absolutely I plan on sticking around. So you better get used to having another brother in the family."

Carlos raised a brow and nodded. "Cocksure of yourself, aren't you? I like him," he told Tomas, watching him slide his hand into Roger's and gaze up at him adoringly.

Pedro grinned. "Of course you do, he's just like you and Mama."

"And speaking of Mama, here she comes with Papa," Carlos said under his breath, and all stood to attention as their parents approached.

"Now that we're all together as a family, introductions need to be officially made," Jenny said and turned to her husband who had stood back watching all that was going on around him earlier and not been introduced. "Spiros, this is Vivian Villiers, Vivian, Carlos's father, Spiros."

"How do you do?" Viv held out her hand to shake.

Spiros accepted it warmly. "I see you make my son happy. Do you plan on getting him *out* of the porn industry?"

"Papa," Carlos murmured.

Viv laughed and rested her arm on Carlos's shoulder. "That will be up to him, but who knows. Once the baby comes along, he may decide to be a stay-at-home dad."

"Mmm," Spiros mumbled, "the men in our family work. There's a job open at the meat shop."

The boys laughed, having had their fair share of years working there.

"No, thanks, Papa, been there, done that, not going back," Carlos told him.

"Mmm, well it's always there if you want to come home," Spiros said, and Jenny introduced him to Angelina.

"My wife was right when she said you are both too young. But then your mother wasn't much older when she met me," he told Pedro. "So we can hardly stop you, just hope and pray that you can do it like we did. And if you ever need help—"

"I'm not coming back to work in the meat shop," Pedro joked, holding up a hand in protest.

"Then we will be here for you both," Spiros continued, watching his youngest son with his even younger new bride-to-be. "Although, I'm sure your father's estate will help you with money to live on," he said to Angelina. "At least you will be financially stable."

"Yes," she said, feeling so small in such a tall family. "I just have to get it sorted out first and hope I have the time while we're here."

"If we can help with that, let us know. We're here for our sons, and so we're here for their partners as well. You will be family soon," Spiros added.

"Thank you," she told him and slid into Pedro's arms. He bent down and rested his head lovingly on hers with a loved-up dopey grin.

Jenny smiled at them for a moment and then slid her left hand through her husband's arm before turning her attention to the last couple. "And this is Roger Dencott, Tomas's partner," she introduced him as Spiros's head twitched. "Be nice," she murmured.

Carlos and Pedro were on guard. There was no way they'd let their father, or any other member of their family, disrespect one of them. They'd fight to the death to love and defend. That's what their mother had taught them.

Tomas's stomach clenched in fear at Spiros's penetrating gaze, and Roger squeezed his hand for support before taking a deep breath to prepare himself.

"Roger," Spiros murmured through gritted teeth. "Apparently, I need to be nice, which is why my wife is digging her nails into my arm. Ow, that's enough." He swatted Jenny's hand away and got a sharply raised brow and pursed lips in return. Turning his head back to his son, he said, "While I raised my sons to be strong, independent, and respectful Greek boys, and then men, and to prepare for the day they met and married a nice Greek girl, obviously, that's not going to happen with you."

He stared at Tomas who stood sick, terrified, and hunched over, almost as if he was about to vomit.

Seeing that terror, his heart painfully went out to him, knowing what it was like to be abandoned and disowned by a father. But he would not do that. He would not be like *his* father and grandfather. He would not continue the hatred and anger over choices his sons made. And he was going to make sure his sons knew that they had his love and support no matter what their choices were, as long as they were the right ones. It was a hard lesson he had only *very* recently learned.

Taking Tomas by the arms as tears flowed down his son's cheeks; he stood toe to toe and eye to eye, matching his son in every physical way. "Oh, Tomas," he murmured. "You are my son, Tomas, and I love you no matter what. Even if that means no wife or children." After an agonising moment he looked at Roger, the tears flowing down his face too. "Do you love my son, Mr Dencott?"

"Yes," Roger managed through his tears.

"Then if you *ever* hurt him, I *will* kill you. Do you understand me?" Spiros put a hand on his shoulder and squeezed for good measure to show Roger he was deadly serious.

Jenny and the boys tensed as tears fell down their own faces.

"Loud and clear, Mr Stephanopoulos," Roger told him, quaking in his shoes. "But I *never* will. He is the man I love and will love forever. I will *never* hurt him. And *that* is a promise."

"Good," Spiros said. "I expect you to stick to that promise, because if you don't, I will hunt you down. And considering what the family business is…and I own a butcher shop..." He raised a brow in acknowledgement and turned back to Tomas, kissing both soaking wet tear-stained cheeks. "You're my son, your happiness is all that matters."

Tomas collapsed into his arms and sobbed while his father held him tight. Jenny, Pedro and Carlos crowded round in a big family hug, hugging each other and crying.

Jenny kissed Spiros on the cheek. "Thank you," she whispered.

He gazed lovingly at his wife. "It's not like I had a choice." He pulled back and motioned to Roger and the girls. "Come, you are family now." Viv moved to Carlos's side and Angelina to Pedro's. Roger slid his arms around Tomas, kissing him on the temple as they all crowded in for a hug.

Everyone else was watching the scene in amusement, huddled together on the sofas, crying and dabbing their eyes. Connie had been catching up on all the gossip with Bette, Bertha and Willow, discussing the differences between the three boys and their appendages. Bertha told them all about Luiz and Tomas's affair with him, and Connie regaled them with stories of how Carlos had her night after night, and what his magic wand could do before it was owned by Viv.

Spiros heard them and finally kicked them out. "Enough," he roared, releasing himself from his family's clutches to walk over to the door and hold it wide open for the women. He didn't want to hear about his son's packages, even though he was proud of the size of the jewels that clearly ran in the family, but other people didn't need to discuss it in front of him. "It's time to go ladies. Goodbye."

He waved an arm toward the door as the women glanced at each other with startled expressions before realising their time was up. They gathered their things and left with cheery goodbyes and waves of sparkle covered hands. He closed the door and quietness befell them.

Finally, the family had peace and quiet, and Jenny led Angelina and Viv to a sofa as two of the boys gathered on the floor in front of their partners.

Pedro sat between Angelina's legs, gazing adoringly up at her, and after she'd gently removed her arm from the sling, sat there kissing the newly placed ring on her hand.

Carlos sat on the floor beside Viv, as she lovingly stroked his hair. He crossed his legs and rested his head on the sofa seat, staring up into her eyes as she lightly slid her fingers along his forehead.

Tomas and Roger shared a huge sofa chair, with Tomas recovering from his father's blessing by happily sliding over the arm and into Roger's lap, giving him a quick kiss before settling down.

Roger wrapped his arms around him in return, and Tomas laid his head on his chest and closed his eyes, weary from everything that had happened. The poisoning, the kidnapping, and the long journey back home. With his stomach full of good Greek food and good medication, he rested, for he had forever with Roger, and knew that in his arms was the place he wanted to be. Always.

Jenny smiled at the happiness her children were in, feeling it emanate around the room. It was quiet, calming, and she knew her boys would never be happier than they all were at that moment with the people they loved.

Spiros sat quietly, gazing at his children and soon to be in-laws. His boys were finally happy with partners they loved. Even Tomas. And how could he deny his son that? He couldn't and didn't want to. Even if it *was* with a man, Tomas was his own man and knew what he wanted. How could he stand in the way of his son's happiness? He couldn't, and wouldn't. Especially after what he had experienced with his own father. He was not about to put that emotional hell on his own sons.

He looked at his wife, the woman who had given him three strong manly sons, and saw happiness radiating out of her. She finally had two daughters, and now two grandchildren on the way as well, and he knew she would revel in wedding plans and baby showers. She was happy, and it showed in every way. The boys had gotten her emotional strength, and she'd fought hard for them.

She'd fought hard when they had left, one by one, when he had given up. And that shamed him; the fact he'd given up so readily when she believed so readily. The fact he had not believed his sons or put their welfare first. The fact that he had done what his father had. Disowned them. So readily.

And it was all down to a man that had ruined every member of his family's life. So readily. And now he was dead, and he was glad.

There was a knock at the door, and the quiet conversations stopped, interrupted once more. Spiros went to answer it, and Giorgio was wheeled into the room. "You're just in time for the family," Spiros told him. "Boys, come and say hello to your great-grandfather."

Everyone in the room looked on in shock. Even Jenny hadn't seen Giorgio in many a year. The boys all looked at her for confirmation as the old man was placed on the other side of the coffee table opposite her. She finally turned to them with a slight nod, and all three slowly rose from their positions and moved around the table to the man in the wheelchair.

Their great-grandfather.

A man they had never spoken to.

Until today.

Spiros nodded his encouragement, standing by his grandfather's side as Giorgio's helper left the room. He held out a hand to Carlos who was first in line. "Carlos, meet your great-grandfather, Giorgio."

Carlos looked from his father to the man in front of him, unsure of what to do. What he *needed* to do. What was required of him. With a glance behind him at his mother, who nodded again, he bent down and kissed his grandfather on both cheeks, allowing Giorgio to lay a gentle hand on both of his, as he gazed into his eyes.

"Ah," Giorgio said. "So blue, just like your mother's. And such a strapping young man. More Australian than Greek, but that's just as good."

"Grandfather," Carlos murmured and pulled back. He stepped aside for Tomas, staying close in case he needed help.

Tomas awkwardly bent down the same as his brother, and kissed the man on both cheeks. "Grandfather."

"Tomas," he said, holding his face in his hands and studying it closely. "You look exactly like my Giorgio, your grandfather. So much like him, so much like your father." He glanced from Tomas to Spiros and back. "So much like them you could be reincarnated." He reluctantly let go so Tomas could step aside, aided by Carlos so Pedro could step up.

"Pedro," he said as his youngest bent down to kiss him.

Pedro had no idea what this was all about and certainly didn't remember ever meeting the man before him. "Grandfather."

"You have the eyes of your mother, and the hair of your father," Giorgio said, eyeing the young man-child before him. "Still a boy, not yet a man."

Pedro grinned softly. "I disagree."

Giorgio smiled. "I'm sure you do. We are Greek. Greek men aren't gay, they're manly and masculine and straight." His laugh was raspy as the boys reluctantly finished the sentence with him.

Tomas looked at Carlos who had his arm around his waist, then glanced at Pedro as he stood up beside him. It was a sentence they no longer wanted to hear.

"Why don't you boys take your seats," Spiros said. "We have some talking to do."

The boys traded glances again and walked around the coffee table to their mother. Carlos perched on the armrest beside her, putting his hand protectively on her left one. Tomas slid down to the floor between her legs, and Pedro sat back in front of Angie, but slid his arm over his mother's legs and around Tomas's shoulder. Tomas put his hand on Pedro's to complete the protection.

Roger and Vivian looked at them in surprise, surprised that they had not resumed their original seats, but Giorgio knew better, and Jenny did too.

She slid her hands over her sons and hung on, going into Mama Bear mode, ready to fight to the death if she had to. And she knew her sons. She had raised them to not only look out for each other, but their parents as well. And she always knew they would rally around her and defend her to the death. They would always be her boys.

And Giorgio knew it as he smiled. "Yes, look at them," he told Spiros who had taken his seat. "They are protecting their mother the way they should. Good Greek boys protect their mothers." He waved a withered finger in their direction. "Good Greek boys who didn't deserve what happened to them."

"Stefano is dead!" Jenny spat. "Absolutely dead?" She needed to know for certain.

Giorgio nodded. "Yes. He is finally gone and will never harm you or the boys ever again."

"Long time coming," Jenny replied. "Look at what they, what *we*, had to put up with because you didn't sort him out years ago." The fire stirred in her belly.

"Hush, now," Spiros warned her.

Giorgio nodded and bowed his head in shame. "No, no, Spiros, she has a right to be angry. She is right. I should have taken care of that man years ago. Maybe then my great-grandsons would not have gone through…" He broke off, weak and tired and old. "We must clear some things up." He gazed at his grandson. "Spiros, we must sort this out once and for all. I am not for this Earth much longer, and the family business needs to be dealt with."

"I want nothing to do with it." Spiros leant back in his chair. "My father told me nearly thirty years ago if I left Greece I would be disowned. I did, and I was. I only came back when Papa died, and Mama needed help. But she has been gone for many years now, and we have done well. We don't want anything."

Giorgio nodded. "That's why I have done what I've done, so you and the boys will not be responsible for any of it anymore."

Jenny frowned out of curiosity as the boys looked from him to her. "What have you done, Giorgio?"

Giorgio gazed at her with weary brown eyes. His hair had long gone, his body long given out on him, but his mind was hanging on. "I have given the family business away."

Spiros frowned in surprise. "What? What do you mean, given it away?"

"Well…" Giorgio turned to him. "I've actually sold it off. I've sold each part off to the highest bidder and was paid well for each of them. The money will be yours if you want it, but if not, it will be given to charities instead. There is nothing left of the family business. That's what makes what Stefano did so ironic. There was no family business left. I had already sold it off before all of this happened."

Spiros eyed his grandfather for a long moment before finally speaking. "We don't want the money." He glanced at Jenny and saw her frown was just as deep and thoughtful as his.

"Yes, I thought as much." Giorgio glanced around the room at everyone in it. Oh, how times had changed, and he had missed so much. "Then I will have my lawyers donate the money upon my death." He turned back to Spiros. "I am so sorry your father did what he did. We argued over that many times. His disowning you. I reminded him that his ancestors came here many a moon ago, but he didn't care. He was stubborn…just like me, and clearly just like you. You take after him, Spiros." He eyed his grandson. "Not just in looks, but in demeanour, temper, anger and passion for women." He glanced at his great-grandsons. "And it looks like your sons have followed you."

He watched Jenny's face and the range of emotions fly over it. "I am so sorry, Jenny. Sorry that we have been apart all these years. Sorry that I never got to talk to my great-grandsons until today. Sorry that you were not welcomed into what was left of the family. Sorry that Stefano did what he did. It was, *and is,* all my fault."

"Do you want forgiveness?" Jenny asked, wondering what point he was trying to make.

Giorgio sighed and bowed his head again. "I don't

know. Forgiveness, absolution, I have no idea. I did nothing to help the situation, and I'm sorry."

Jenny sighed and relaxed. While she had only met Giorgio twice upon her moving to Mykonos, she had found him pleasant. But the issue between her husband and his family had taken a toll on everyone. Including her sons. She didn't like it one little bit, and it had to stop. "Giorgio. The next generation of Stephanopouloses are coming. I don't know whether you'll make it to see them born, but you should at least know, and meet the ones who have captured your grandsons' hearts." She placed a hand on Angelina's shaking arm. "You would know of Angelina Poulos, Andros's daughter. She and Pedro are now engaged with a child on the way." She glanced at Angie then Giorgio. "Angelina, your great-grandfather-in-law-to-be, Giorgio Stephanopoulos."

Angelina blinked, stared at Jenny, then Pedro, who was looking up at her, to finally look at the withered old man in the wheelchair. "Um…hello."

Giorgio nodded with a secret smile. "We were already related once…long ago. Your father was Stefano's stepson at one time, but we have never met." He glanced at Pedro's face, taking in him and his fiancée behind him. "Both so young," he muttered. "Both so young."

"That's what we said," Jenny told him. "But we are here for them both and will help as much as we can." She turned her attention to Vivian. "And this is Vivian Villiers, Carlos's fiancée and a mother-to-be." She waved a hand at Viv who tried to look cool and calm.

"Hello," she said to Giorgio. "Nice to meet you."

"Well, look at you. Carlos, my boy, you've got yourself a fine-looking woman there," Giorgio told his great-grandson.

Carlos flushed and looked from his great-grandfather to Viv to his mother.

"And in the chair is Roger Dencott, Tomas's partner." She tensed. For she had been told many, many times that Greek men were not gay, or took gay lovers. *Regardless* of what Greek history actually said.

Giorgio studied the squirming Roger and turned to Spiros. "Have *you* accepted him?"

Spiros took a deep breath and looked from Giorgio to Roger to Tomas on the floor between his mother's legs. "For the sake of my son, I have. I will not do to him what my father did to me," he told Giorgio. "I will not do what my father did and disown my children for the choices they make." He looked at all three of his sons protecting their mother as they rightfully should.

Giorgio nodded at Spiros's words and glanced from Tomas to Roger back to Tomas. "Are you happy, Tomas?"

Tomas glanced from his father to his great-grandfather. "Yes."

Giorgio nodded again. "Then that's all that matters." He turned to Roger. "You take good care of him, young man. You do realise what the family business is, right?"

Roger nodded fearfully, praying to God he didn't get the same speech from his lover's great-grandfather that he had from his father. "Yes, sir. I've been told."

"Good, good." Giorgio's head moved up and down

slowly. "Then we must finish up before time runs out." Turning back to Spiros he said, "are you absolutely sure you want nothing to do with the family money?"

"Absolutely," Spiros said. "I want nothing to do with it."

Giorgio laid a finger on his chin. "Then it will be given away. The house has been sold off, as all the buildings have. There is nothing but money, and that will go soon. Now," he glanced at Jenny, "with Stefano being gone and him having no children, that means his estate goes to his only living heirs."

Spiros frowned. "He has none. My aunt is dead, his second wife and fiancée are all dead. Andros was only his stepson. He has no heirs."

Giorgio raised his brows in surprise. "Besides us… you mean…"

"What?" Spiros frowned. "But we aren't his heirs. We stopped being related when Aunt Marishka died."

Giorgio chuckled. "Yes, but his only living legal heirs happen to be the man who was his father-in-law and the man who was his nephew, along with his three sons, of course, because his wife died while they were still married."

"They inherit the Papadopoulos estate." Jenny's eyes narrowed and she tilted her head. "My boys inherit the estate?"

"Well," Giorgio said, "I don't want it or need it. Spiros…what about you?"

Spiros waved his hands in defiance. "Don't want it, get rid of it, it is nothing to do with us."

Jenny had been quickly thinking about the

information and what it meant, with a million thoughts racing through her mind.

"Jenny?" Giorgio spied the look on her face and knew what it meant.

Spiros turned to her. "We *are not* taking one cent from that man or his estate."

A strange sound came from Jenny's throat as her head turned slightly. "Well…"

"Mama?" Carlos asked, looking down at her from his position on the arm of the sofa. "What are you thinking?"

Tomas and Pedro looked up at her, equally strange looks on their faces.

"Well…" Jenny finally looked at Spiros and Giorgio. "After what that bastard did to my children and me the irony of them ending up with that bastard's estate is too glorious to let go. He owes us," she spat. "*He owes us big time.* And if inheriting the estate and everything he had is the consequence of his actions then I say we take it." She gripped her sons' hands, hanging on for grim death. The thought of spending that bastard's money on frivolous things for herself and her children, the ones he called half-breeds all these years, plus the future grandchildren, was just too good to pass up. And there was no way she was going to do that.

"Jenny…" Spiros said. "You can't be serious?" He couldn't believe his wife wanted to take Stefano Papadopoulos's estate after everything he'd done.

"Oh, the hell I can't be," she snapped, staring her husband in the eye. "After what he did to *our* sons, just the thought of inheriting what was his is delicious. After all, *he* wanted nothing to do with us. *He* wanted to *kill* our children. Or have you forgotten what he did to them already?"

Spiros blanched. "*Of course* I haven't, but it just seems…wrong…strange," he said.

"Maybe," she relented. "But the irony is too much to dismiss." She looked Giorgio square in the eye. "Can your lawyers sell off everything he owns so just the money is left? Like what you did with your estate. And then we'll take the money and *blow it* on everything we've ever wanted."

The vengeful tone of her voice made him smile. He saw what Spiros had seen in this woman and silently applauded her for her tenacity. "I'll have my lawyer deal with it when he deals with mine," he told her, watching her eyes travel from each of her sons to her husband, pleading with them to understand her reasoning. He glanced at Spiros to see if it had worked.

Spiros was studying his wife's eyes, looking for the decision behind her choice. He didn't understand it, and sure as hell didn't like it, but knew she must have a reason for it. While he wanted nothing to do with either his grandfather or ex-uncle, he knew that Jenny was thinking of revenge, and that revenge was going to be delicious for her. So, how could he deny his wife that after everything that had happened?

Giorgio saw the understanding dawn in Spiros's eyes and knew that they were a match made in heaven. The Greek and the Australian. A match that no one would ever come between.

Spiros sighed. "If it is what you want, my love," he told the love of his life. "Then it's what we shall do."

Jenny smiled at her husband, then Giorgio, then her sons and future in-laws. None of them knew of her plans. *Of course* they didn't. For she was just formulating them as she sat there listening to the menfolk make all the decisions. But she had made hers, and if it was one thing she knew, revenge, even though her enemy was now dead in his grave, was going to be oh so deliciously sweet.

About the Author

L.J. has been writing since 2006, when her first of many novels, ***The Road To Vegas,*** was born. In 2016 she created the ***Porn Star Brothers*** series about three sizzlingly hot Australian born Greek Island raised brothers who became the hottest porn stars in '70s America.

L.J. lives in Australia, loves '80s music, disaster movies, and collecting Jackie Collins books as Jackie is her inspiration and mentor.

L.J. Diva is the adult pen name for author Tiara King. You can find more about Tiara on her website; follow her on social media, or visit her publishing house, Royal Star Publishing.

Socials

tiaraking.com.au/ljdiva

royalstarpublishing.com.au

Sign up for *Tiara's* Newsletter…

Make sure you're always in the know and never miss free exclusives, the latest news, book updates, and so much more with newsletters from…

tiaraking.com.au

Have you read these?

THE PORN STAR BROTHERS SERIES

Carlos: Book 1
Pedro: Book 2
Tomas: Book 3
Retribution: Book 4
Porn Star Brothers
Forever
Love Never Dies
Stefan: The New Generation
DeLuca
Spiros & Jenny
And Always

THE ILLICIT THINGS SERIES

Her
Him
Madam X

A NOVEL INVESTIGATION SERIES

Designs in Crime
A Killer Plot
Murder on the Set
A Novel Investigation (omnibus)

Or these?

NOVELS

Burning Desires
Anything for You
Falling for London
The Road to Vegas
Hollywood Dreams
The Billionaire's Dirty Little Secret

SHORT STORIES

The Body
The Perfect Plot
The Star of Your Own Crime Scene